# "*I will,*" Haze said

"You—will what?"

"I will marry you."

Lori stared. "You said no before."

"I'm more desperate than I thought."

"You said you wouldn't do it even if all your family were thrown on the streets," she reminded him. "You'd rather be hand-cuffed to an iceberg."

"All true. But I need the money," he said flatly. "You were right—it's a damned good deal. Besides—"

Never had she been so right, so often—and felt so bad about it. "Besides, what?"

Haze Callahan slanted a smoky look at her. "Icebergs eventually melt."

*ANN CHARLTON* wanted to be a commercial artist but became a secretary. She wanted to play the piano but plays guitar instead, and she never planned to be a writer. From time to time she abseils, which surprises her because she is afraid of heights. Born in Sydney, Ann now lives in Brisbane. She would like to do more tapestry work and paint miniatures and has absolutely no plans to research a book in the Amazon or to learn to play the bouzouki.

## Books by Ann Charlton

HARLEQUIN PRESENTS
1319—LOVE SPIN
1777—HOT NOVEMBER
1782—STEAMY DECEMBER

# ANN CHARLTON

## Married to the Man

# Harlequin Books

TORONTO • NEW YORK • LONDON
AMSTERDAM • PARIS • SYDNEY • HAMBURG
STOCKHOLM • ATHENS • TOKYO • MILAN
MADRID • WARSAW • BUDAPEST • AUCKLAND

ISBN 0-373-11892-9

MARRIED TO THE MAN

First North American Publication 1997.

# CHAPTER ONE

SHE saw the cameras ahead and found one last surge of energy to raise her shuffling feet and cross the finishing line in a sprint. It was more pride than energy, for she was exhausted. Sheer pride, too, that kept her on her feet as a television reporter and cameraman hurried alongside.

'And just finishing the Canberra Marathon in *great* style is Lorelei Tate, senior executive with the Tate Corporation in Melbourne, and it's pretty obvious why her family calls her Wonderwoman. Is there anything this little gal can't do?

'As a university student she won every academic prize that was going, she's Tate's youngest director—and the only woman on the board—and she works out and trains for marathons in her spare time. Great! Hello there, Lorelei . . . today's time was short of your personal best, but you must be pretty pleased with it anyway. How do you feel?'

'This little gal' had just run twenty-six miles; her muscles felt as if they were melting, her pulses hammered in her head and her breathing sounded like a broken accordion being squeezed. But she managed a smile for the critical camera and gasped, 'Fine.'

Pride again. She had lied. This time there wasn't even the euphoria of crossing the line to make the gruelling effort worthwhile. Once, the act itself had been achievement enough, but now she felt oddly disappointed as she looked around at the cheering onlookers, and the runners warming down while they seriously discussed the secrets of their pre-race diets and their biorhythms and PBs. She'd run the race, but what was at the end of it?

Other runners were crossing the finish but the reporter stuck with her, and she wished him to the devil. All she wanted to do was collapse in a heap and groan out her pain. But she couldn't do that. She was Lori Tate of the iron will. She had trained herself to stay cool in public, do her crying in private.

Wonderwoman—a title bestowed on her in mockery by her brother and cousins, but one she had subsequently earned. Unfortunately, the Tate men had a few other names for her. The Hex. Jinx. Lori preferred not to remember how she had come by those.

'Great! And I just have to ask you, Lorelei—*what* spare time? How does a woman with your responsibilities find time for training?'

By cutting down on sleep. By driving herself out to the gym or onto the road before breakfast, or after ten or twelve hours in the office or on site. By giving up most social engagements except those related to business. 'Oh,' she wheezed to the camera, 'always find time for things that are important.'

'Great!' he said again, and patted her shoulder. 'What you need now, Lorelei, is a long, cool drink.' And he flaunted a can bearing the name of one of the race sponsors.

'What you need...' Lori bent at the hips to ease the cramps in her lower abdomen. Her male relatives had been saying that to her for years. 'What you need, Lorelei, is a sense of humour.' 'What you need, Lorelei, is to loosen up.' 'What you need, Lorelei, is to be more flexible.' Usually this advice came when she disagreed with them, or pressed for the same benefits that male Tates took for granted.

'What you need, Lorelei, is a man,' her own brother had had the nerve to tell her when she had demanded her place on the board as co-inheritor of their father's shares. 'You're getting sour and aggressive.' Since Woody's will had been read, though, Mark had been distinctly pleased that she didn't have a man. Even triumphant.

Lori accepted a drink from a race volunteer. She felt the pang of loss again at the thought of Woody. Eventually, she knew from experience, she would become accustomed to this new empty space in her life. Just now, though, she still had to remind herself that it would never be Woody's voice she would hear when she answered the phone, that Woody would not greet her at the door of the old house with the lilies run wild.

The pain of loss was not the only hurt. Woody, whom she'd loved, whose house had been the real home of her childhood, had been the one person in the world who had understood her, had known how hard she'd worked for her place in the scheme of things, how she valued her independence. Woody had loved her, respected her talent and capabilities, or so she had thought.

The sting of betrayal was as harsh as her physical pain. Woody was Mark's godmother as well as Lori's, and she'd left the house of Lori's childhood to Mark, who had no special feelings for it. Solely to Mark. Unless...

'Unless I marry before I turn thirty,' Lori said a few days later in Fairlie Tate's studio. Her cousin's artist wife had transformed Carson's formerly stuffy house in Toorak, which now smelled of oil paint and linseed oil and turps and was the better for it. 'If I do, I inherit her house and things. If I don't—it goes to Mark.'

Fairlie, on hands and knees, brushing size over another massive canvas for her coming exhibition, shook her head in commiseration.

'That inner city area has been re-zoned,' Lori went on, 'and Mark is already making plans to demolish the house and sell her wonderful garden to a developer for an office block site!'

'Maybe he won't.'

'He will. Chalk up another victory for Mark.' Lori sighed and turned away to pour some coffee from the pot on the warmer. 'He's still crowing over his last win. I put my weight behind a brilliant woman for the vacant seat on the board, but Mark's candidate got the appointment. Competent, but nothing special. But a man, of course, who belongs to all the right clubs and speaks the right language.'

Fairlie wrinkled her nose. 'I heard.'

'Men,' Lori declared, looking at Fairlie's abstract paintings stacked along the wall, '*negotiate* to advance their careers. Women *carp*. Men discuss the flaws in a colleague's performance. Women bitch about people behind their backs. Men wear grey suits and blue shirts and the same haircut for ever and no one comments, but a woman is considered unnatural if *she* prefers suits and keeps one hairstyle because it's functional and businesslike.'

Fairlie slanted a look at Lori's excellent burgundy suit and her light brown hair, drawn back firmly into a knot. 'You could have a change now and then, I suppose.'

'I don't have *time* to shop for every new fashion and to change hairstyles. I have to compete with men who never have to waste time worrying if their lipstick is fresh, or if their tights are laddered or their slip is showing.' She sat down with her coffee and crossed her legs, then quickly uncrossed them again. 'Ever since Sharon whatsername did it in that movie, any woman has to think twice even about how she crosses her legs!'

Fairlie laughed, but looked sharply at the coffee-cup trembling ever so slightly in Lori's hands. By way of distraction, Lori asked about Carson. Her eldest cousin was currently commuting between Melbourne and the Colussus headquarters in Brisbane, which he ran for the Tate Group.

'And how's junior?' she went on.

Fairlie eased onto her haunches and slid a hand over the very pregnant belly under her outsized shirt. 'Kicking beautifully. Only two months to go. Carson's ecstatic. I never thought he would be so delighted. After all, he's been through it all before with David. David's over the moon too—he can't wait to have a stepbrother or sister.'

It was bound to be a step*brother*, Lori thought, fatalistically. The family was top heavy with males, who all took up their natural places in the business and got all the best views. She finished her coffee, poured another.

'How much coffee do you drink in a day?'

Lori shrugged.

'Your hands are shaking. And I'll bet you're not sleeping—there are bags under your eyes.'

'OK—there are bags under my bags,' Lori said with a weak smile.

'You know what they call this, don't you? Burn-out.'

Lori gave a ragged laugh. 'No, I can't have burn-out. Men have burn-out. Women have *nervous breakdowns*.' She shuddered, imagining her nervous breakdown being discussed in corridors, in the boardroom. 'Poor Lorelei...the pressure's fierce at the top. You can't expect a woman to take it like a man. We always knew she would crack one day,'

Fairlie propped the newly stretched canvas against the wall.

'Lori—what you need is a holiday.'

'What you need...' Lori felt a surge of anger at the phrase, but was too tired to sustain it.

'And I don't mean one of those overseas dashes you do to run in marathons in every smoke-filled, polluted city you can find. Where was it last time? Tokyo?'

'I haven't got time for a real holiday,' Lori said, waving a hand jerkily. She knocked the coffee-cup against a shelf and it hurtled to the floor. Splashes of black dregs appeared on her excellent suit. She looked down at the mess, noticed there was a run in her tights. Her throat went tight. 'These were new this morning!' she said on a rising note. 'How come we can invent machines to take photographs of Venus but we can't invent tights that will last a lousy twenty-four hours?'

Her voice echoed up to the studio skylights, high and hysterical. Lori stared at Fairlie in consternation.

'A holiday,' Fairlie said emphatically. 'And the sooner the better. You'd better let me organise it for you. Somewhere quiet where you can let your hair down. But somewhere you could have some fun,' she went on, with the air of someone prescribing medication. 'Somewhere you could possibly meet a terrific man—'

Lori sliced her hand through the air. 'No men. Not unless you can come up with a convenient male who'll marry me before August to wipe the smirk off Mark's face, then fade obediently into the background while I get on with my life.'

Fairlie's smile was complacent, almost pitying. She didn't know any men like that. 'How about an island—in the tropics?'

'An island.' The very phrase had a calming effect. Quiet, remote. 'Yes, an island—uninhabited, preferably. Do you know anywhere like that?'

'I know someone who does. Leave it to me. Could you rough it in a tent? Of course you could,' Fairlie ironically answered herself. 'You beat the Tate boys on all those Outward Bound things, didn't you?'

A tent. The simple life. No complications. No mirrors. No tights. No stupid, hurtful legal clauses. No men. Lori already felt passionately attached to the idea of a tent on an island.

She went north to her quiet place in the sun two weeks later. Fairlie had found her an uninhabited island with a tent already on it. A boat would deliver her to this paradise and leave new provisions and fresh water on the beach at intervals.

So soothed was Lori by the prospect of her holiday, that she had only mildly objected to having a small task foisted on her by The Uncles. Would she look over a piece of property adjoining some Tate land-holdings on the Queensland coast quite near to her destination? they had asked. The owner, Callahan, would probably sell, but he demanded a rendezvous with a Tate director as a preliminary. As it would delay her departure to the island by only four hours or so, she agreed.

Of course, 'quite near' turned out to be some forty-five minutes' drive from the coast, and she'd had to hire a car for the journey.

In the tiny office of Callahan's Survival School a man with very little hair introduced himself as Tom and told her that Mr Callahan was running late because he'd been called out, and she'd have to wait if she wanted him to drive her to the property. To all her subsequent queries and objections, he simply shrugged and grinned and checked out her legs.

Once she had viewed the displayed photographs of enthusiasts scaling cliffs and fording rivers, read a poster about making safe fires, leafed through four illustrated survival manuals written by H. Callahan and inspected a display of climbing harnesses, she had exhausted the amenities of the office. She went outside and walked along the hot, deserted main street of the tiny hinterland town.

In Melbourne the early May weather had turned decidedly wintry, but up here in the tropics summer persisted. Mr Callahan was now over an hour late.

She shaded her eyes as a puff of dust heralded some movement on the road at last. A four-wheel-drive vehicle hurtled into view and performed a screeching loop to park outside the strung together shops. A tall man got out and powered across the footpath in strides so fast that he was almost at the steps of the Callahan office before the slam of his car door came like a gunshot.

Lori winced. This must be Callahan himself. And moving not so much like a man in a hurry as a man in a temper. Lori closed her eyes and thought of her island, then walked back and entered the office.

'. . . not here. She's gone for a walk,' Lori heard Tom say from behind a closed door. 'A bit of a dragon lady— used to giving orders, I reckon—doesn't like being kept waiting. But then, she's a Tate.'

There was a grunt in reply, then a curious buzzing noise that blocked out the voices and the noise of her own footsteps as she moved further inside. The buzzing ceased.

'No joy from the tax department, eh? Are we out of business, then, boss?' It was Tom again.

'They've given us the maximum time to pay, which means we can keep going another month or two. If I ever get my hands on that accountant—' the other man said in a voice so surly he had no need to finish the sentence.

'What you need is a win in the lottery. Or a rich widow—a rich woman anyway...'

That phrase again. What you need . . . Lori almost felt sorry for the unseen Callahan. Even sorrier for any rich widows in the vicinity. She raised her hand to knock at the door but was stayed by the sound of her own name.

'Take this Lorelei Tate,' Tom went on with a snicker. 'You might as well—nobody else has.'

Oh, very amusing! Lori knocked at the door but a burst of buzzing masked the sound and then Tom's voice went on. 'Thirtyish, I reckon. Real serious hair, brass buttons and career shoulder-pads. Clever kind of eyes that give you the shivers and a handshake cold enough to give you frostbite. I reckon you'd have to lie back and think of the Bank of England.'

There were some male guffaws at this tremendous wit.

'Terrible name—Lorelei.' As an afterthought Tom added, 'Eyes are a nice grey and her legs aren't bad, though.'

'It wouldn't be a total sacrifice, then,' said Callahan, and she could almost *hear* his grin.

There was more sniggering from Tom. Lori scowled and absently chafed her perpetually cold hands. Arrogant swine, discussing her as if she were a piece of merchandise just waiting to be plucked off the shelf by some self-satisfied man. She waited for the next burst of buzzing to pass, then knocked again.

Tom peered out. 'Ah—g'day, Miss Tate. Me and Callahan were just talking about you,' the man had the nerve to say. 'Wondered where you'd got to.'

'There really *is* a Callahan, then?' she said tartly. 'I do hope to see some evidence soon that he's not a figment of your imagination. I have a boat to catch.'

'I'm Callahan.'

The evidence was plentiful, garbed in faded army fatigues, and crowded into the doorway. A tall man, broad in shoulder and chest, long in the legs and a figment of no one's imagination unless you were in advertising, dreaming up hard-bitten outdoor types to sell beer to soft city people.

He had taken up a leaning position against one side of the doorway, an arm extended across, the hand flat on the other side of the frame. But it was no casual, relaxed stance, more like someone wedging open a narrowing exit. Or a man trying to prevent the roof falling in. His eyes were shaded by the brim of a cap but Lori saw them flick over her.

He clicked a small electric shaver closed and dropped it into his pocket then pushed off from the doorframe, extending his hand with a marked lack of enthusiasm. Maybe he was the kind of man who was uncomfortable shaking hands with a woman. Or maybe he was anticipating frostbite.

Lori took his hand, had a brief experience of suppressed strength and warm calluses. 'I'm a busy person, Mr Callahan. I would have appreciated a call to let me know just how late you were going to be,' she said, mildly enough considering how long she'd waited.

Callahan's mouth thrust forward. His temper had not cooled, she saw, in spite of all that jokiness with Tom at her expense.

'Next time I'll bring a note from my mother. Shall we go?' His feet were shod in heavy hiking boots that thumped on the timber floor. He lifted his cap and ran a large hand over his forehead and on over the back of his head.

The man had long hair. It was bound neatly enough into a tail at the base of his neck, almost concealed by his collar, but Lori didn't like long hair on men. She always had a mental picture of a man gathering up his hair to slip a band on it, and the image was relentlessly feminine.

He pulled open the door and turned suddenly, and she was caught staring at the back of his neck. His eyes narrowed a fraction and he made an impatient 'after you' gesture with one hand, as if he had picked up her silent derision but couldn't care less. Not a man to court a prospective buyer.

The door shut behind them and he strode ahead to the four-wheel-drive.

'Mr Callahan—unless your temper has improved, I'm not predisposed to get into that vehicle with you driving.'

He had the passenger door open and turned his head toward her in disbelief.

'I saw you drive in,' she went on drily. 'I'm just about to take my first holiday for three years, and I do so want to *live*. I have a hire car. We'll take that.'

She pointed to the sedan.

'There are fifteen-odd miles of unsealed road before we even get to my gates, and it's roughed up with washouts from the rain last week,' he informed her. 'As I'm not *predisposed* to dig your dandy little hire car out of a pothole, it's my car or none.'

Her own temper began to fray. 'You're a rude man, Mr Callahan.'

'Sorry, ma'am,' he drawled, in a tone lacking apology. 'It's been a difficult morning.'

Lori considered her position. She looked at her watch, then at Callahan. 'Seriously, are you fit to drive?'

He looked unblinkingly at her. 'What makes you think I might not be?'

'You turn up late, bad-tempered, baggy-eyed, shaving at the last minute—are you suffering from a hangover?'

He left the passenger door open, went around the other side.

'No hangover, Ms Tate. If you want to go, get in. If not, goodbye.'

She was tempted to forget the whole thing, but she had already wasted so much time and was unwilling that it should all be for nothing. She got in. Her straight suit skirt gave her some trouble as she negotiated the high step and slid into the seat. As she pulled her skirt down to cover her knees she felt Callahan's eyes on her legs. She wondered if she had another run in her tights. Or if he would agree with Tom that her legs weren't bad. As if she cared either way.

'What kind of a place are you expecting?' he asked. 'You've come dressed for a stroll around a city plaza.'

'Mr Callahan,' she said briskly, clasping her hands over the briefcase in her lap, 'this is business and I'm dressed for business. You get me to the property and I'll worry about my dress-code.'

He reached across her to the shelf beneath the dashboard and rummaged in a welter of leather gloves, folded pages of newsprint, empty bread wrappers, drink bottles, binoculars and cameras until he seized the earpiece of a pair of sunglasses. He turned his head to look at Lori as he shook the glasses free, and he was so close that the peak of his cap grazed her forehead.

Dark blue eyes he had, heavily lashed. They lingered on her for a moment, as if they'd discovered something worth a second glance. Or as if he was giving her the chance to fully admire his rugged good looks. Not the kind of male she admired at all, but she conceded that he had a certain basic attraction, in spite of the long hair. Those navy blue eyes were disconcerting, and she moved her head back a little out of range and said, 'You missed a bit, Mr Callahan.'

His mouth turned down at the corners. 'Nope, don't think so. I've seen all I want to see.'

'I'm not talking about the way you're staring.'

'Was I staring?'

'You still are.' She met his gaze levelly, as was her custom. If Callahan got the shivers from the impact of her 'clever' eyes, he hid it well. It was Lori who felt the odd shiver.

'My apologies. I haven't seen a Tate director before. Not in the flesh...' He glanced at her high-buttoned shirt, the long-sleeved linen jacket, and added sardonically, 'So to speak.'

'I am not typical of Tate directors. I'm the only female one, for a start.'

'Yeah, well the female of the species will probably be a hell of a lot more dangerous than the male. And that's bad enough in my experience.'

'Rest easy,' she said wryly. 'Big business is doing everything possible to keep dangerous females out.'

His eyes narrowed at her tone and she regretted letting her bitterness show. To Lori's relief, he shook the sunglasses free and removed himself to his own side of the car to put them on. She shoved some displaced items back onto the dashboard shelf. The sheets of newspapers had crossword puzzles on them with numerous notes and crossings-out in the margins. The newest looking of them was completed, all but the number twenty-eight across.

'"Not in the flesh", you said. Does that mean you've had some dealings with us before?' she asked, and added at his sceptical expression, 'It's a big organisation, Mr Callahan—I don't get to hear everything.'

He started the car. 'You Tates have been after my land ever since the resort boom. Very inventive with your methods of persuasion. I took your property company to court over one of them.'

She looked curiously at him. 'What happened?'

'I won.' He turned the blank lenses of his sunglasses towards her, added sardonically, 'Won the skirmish, lost the war. But don't think you're going to get the land for a pittance. I've got another buyer interested.'

Lori smiled. 'They all say that, Mr Callahan.' She laid her attaché case flat on her lap and opened it, catching at the glossy brochure from the charter boat service Fairlie had booked to slip it under an elastic restraint. Its illustration of an impossibly blue sea and a verdant tropical island seemed more like fantasy than ever sitting in this serviceable vehicle with the rough-edged Callahan.

She selected a file, a notebook and a pen from their respective slots in her neat case and caught Callahan inspecting the orderly lay-out with the amusement she would have expected from someone who drove around with ancient remains of lunches and old crossword puzzles under his nose. She clipped shut the lid of her case. 'Left side of the jaw, below the ear,' she said.

He turned to her, and this time it was not only the sun lenses that looked blank. 'What?'

'The bit you missed,' she explained.

He thought about it for a moment, then tilted his head to look in the rear-view mirror, touched the patch of whiskers that the razor hadn't mown. Lori fancied she heard the faint rasp of fingertips on bristles, but it was unlikely considering the noise the vehicle was making.

His laugh came, low and resonant, and he displayed some very large, very white teeth in a smile that made her sit up straight and pay attention to the fact-file that Mark had given her.

'Perhaps we could dispense with a few queries before we reach the property,' she was saying, when a car overtook them with a flash of silver and several blasts on the horn.

Lori glimpsed the smooth, brown legs of a woman driver in the low sports model. She brought her Mercedes crookedly to a screeching halt at the side of the road and Callahan pulled up behind it. He went through the routine motions of applying the handbrake and turning off the ignition with such hard-jawed deliberation that Lori had half decided this interruption was not welcome.

He was halfway to the other car when its driver leapt out and rushed at him, threw her arms around him and spread her hands on his broad back. She was a voluptuous redhead, probably in her early thirties, with the smooth, tanned legs and arms of a young girl emphasised with two gold anklets and a quantity of gold and silver bangles.

Lori dragged her eyes away and concentrated on her paperwork, made a few notes, but couldn't resist the occasional glance at the pair. Each time she carried back to her work a vivid image. The gleam of sunlight on the enamelled nails of the redhead's hands. The powerful line of Callahan's shoulders, the mass of him, sheltering the woman. Her uptilted face, his downturned. The evocative space between their profiles. His large hand stroking her hair with a tenderness that was oddly moving.

So much for her instincts, Lori thought. The redhead looked very welcome indeed in Callahan's embrace.

Lori inspected her fingernails, checked her tights for runs, stirred the rubble on the dashboard shelf—anything to avoid the romantic tableau outside. She looked up the clue to number twenty-eight across. 'One who gives financial support.'

For heaven's sake, Lori thought, growing irritable as the minutes passed and the two stayed locked together in her peripheral vision. If this foreplay continued they would be loping off into the scrub by the road any minute. She put aside her case and papers and opened the door.

'I hate to interrupt, Mr Callahan,' she said. The woman was nuzzled up close to the left side of his jaw. That unshaven patch of bristles must be murder on her lovely, delicate skin. 'But how long do you think you're likely to be this time?'

The redhead hung onto his arm and walked with him to the vehicle. Lori was startled to see that there were tears on her face even though she was smiling. 'Sorry, it's my fault,' she said to Lori. 'It's not every day you nearly lose your son.' The words appeared to frighten her, and she grasped Callahan's arms again, bunching up the fabric of his shirt as she dug her fingers in. 'Tony could have died up there if you hadn't—hadn't—how can I ever thank you?'

'By making sure the young idiot knows the dangers. I've told him to come to me for some lessons as soon as he gets out of hospital. Don't let him climb again until I've taught him some common sense precautions. And throw out any other old rope you've got lying around.'

'I'll burn it all,' she said fervently. She kissed him soundly on the mouth then relinquished her grip at last.

'See you tonight?' the redhead said as the four-wheel-drive started up.

Callahan hesitated, then nodded. 'I'll drop by about eight. Tony will be fine. Take it easy, Justine.' Through the window Callahan gave her hand a last squeeze. The silver Mercedes took off in front of them and soon after turned into a driveway with lion-topped stone pillars that led to a dazzling ranch-style house.

'How old is Tony?' asked Lori, after a short battle with her curiosity.

'Sixteen.'

'You—rescued him?'

He nodded. 'The fool kid was halfway down a rock-face with a thirty-year-old rope never intended for climbing. Alone. Of all the stupid—' He shook his head. 'Lucky for him his leg got stuck in a crevice and stopped his descent. The rope probably wouldn't have held out till he got all the way down. He's lucky to be in hospital with just a fracture and lacerations.'

'Tom said you were "called out". Are you a rescue volunteer or something?'

'I'm rostered on for a few days a week when I'm around.'

Lori studied his profile. 'A boy might have died if you hadn't been there. Isn't that...? I mean, that must shake you up a bit.'

He showed his teeth. 'Still worried I'm not fit to drive? It's all in the training. I've had to get behind a wheel and drive after far worse than getting one scared kid down to earth. Look.' He held a hand in front of her face. 'Steady as a rock.'

It was too. Strong, square, with a few new scratches and the white lightning flash of an old scar along the thumb. The nails were neat and squared off, half-moons showed at their base. Pity help the incompetent tax accountant if Callahan got these on him. Large, sun-tanned, capable hands—just as at home tenderly stroking a woman's hair as hauling a frightened boy to safety.

Callahan had skills that could mean the difference between life and death. Lori felt a flare of interest and admiration. Callahan's Survival School. She hadn't paid much attention to what that name actually meant.

'You could have told me you'd been out saving someone's life when I accused you of having a hangover.'

He grinned. 'Please, ma'am, I'm late because I had to save a life? Would you have believed me?'

She made a small gesture in acknowledgement. After a short silence she said, 'Justine must have had her son when she was very young.'

Instantly she regretted the comment. There was a certain smugness about the smile that tilted the corners of his mouth. The man probably thought she wanted to find out just what his relationship with the redhead was—as if she could care. It was typical of this big, bold, physical type. Always certain that women were interested in them.

'Nineteen,' he said. 'Lovely woman. She and Tony moved here a few months ago. She runs an art gallery in a resort mall down on the coast—art for discerning tourists. Very successful.'

'A widow?' Lori said snippily. 'Maybe Justine is just what you need. A rich widow. Grateful too.'

His head turned sharply. 'You overheard all that?'

'Some. I suspect I was spared worse by the noise of your morning shave.' She let a few moments pass, and when he made no rejoinder said, 'What, no apology for snickering about me with Tom?'

'If you will listen at closed doors—' He lifted a shoulder and the movement was as eloquent as a French phrase. 'As for Justine, her husband is very much alive—separated from her, but too bloody-minded to give her a divorce. She's having a tough time with young Tony...he's gone a bit wild. What he needs is a man's influence.'

'I dare say,' Lori said, inexplicably irritated again by that phrase. Her tone was caustic. 'This is fascinating, but let's get down to business.'

'Lady, you're the one who's fishing for details,' he drawled, aggravatingly at ease.

He was, she was glad to see, less complacent when she began asking questions about the property. His answers were terse, his frown ferocious. By the time the vehicle had jogged and swayed along the washed out, boggy access road, Callahan was moodily silent.

She saw why soon enough. They passed through a gateway onto land forested with eucalyptus on the upper slopes, thicketed with rainforest in ravines. There was a creek, remnants of a water course that had worn its way over eons through solid rock, narrowing into chasms, broadening into water holes. Around it all was the verdant cloak of plants and vines, and, revelling in it, water birds, ducks and parrots flashing crimson, green and sapphire.

Even before she saw the house, she saw why the idea of selling this place made his black brows meet in the middle and his back muscles stiffen with tension.

His house was a lived-in, rambling affair but not finished. It sat on a rise looking down over a stretch of the creek at the front and projecting over a downslope of rainforest at the back. A pile of old fenceposts bristling with rusty bolts lay in a doorless shed. Stacked alongside them was a pile of windows from old houses. Some of them had already been built into the house, where they caught the sunlight in portholes and triangles of stained glass.

'It's unusual,' Lori said. It had an unassuming, settled kind of look—a sense of peace that drew you in, like Woody's place.

She wondered if he felt the way she did, anticipating the loss of a place she cared about. Like Woody's house, once this property was sold it would be dismantled. With their Japanese investors, Tate's would take out the wild trees and have hundreds of nursery-grown palms planted in their place. The smaller ravines would be smoothed out and turfed, the creek piped underground to a man-made lake rimmed with striped umbrellas and wrought-iron tables.

It was business—some would say progress—and Lori had defended it countless times. But lately she had wondered just how much the world needed another office block, or another resort. Lori discovered a vague feeling of comradeship with Callahan. 'Are you—building it yourself?'

'Was,' he said abruptly. 'I was building another wing so we could accommodate larger classes.'

'You teach here?'

He made a broad gesture that took in all the land around. The whole place was his classroom.

'Are there so many people wanting to learn how to rock-climb, then?' she said.

'I don't run a school for weekend hobbyists, if that's what you're getting at,' he said tersely. 'Australia is a big, empty country, and there are people who need to know how to survive in its rough places—people in mineral exploration, road-crews, long-distance drivers, anthropologists, botanists, film-makers, light aircraft pilots—' He stopped abruptly, then said drily, 'I've been so busy saving lives I haven't had breakfast. You want to come in for some coffee while I eat—or are you too busy for that, Ms Tate?'

'Coffee would be most welcome, Mr Callahan.'

Inside, the house had a spartan beauty. Light flooded in whitely from the glass front and filtered rose, green and gold through recycled stained glass panels. Some of the fenceposts had been transformed into the warm, smooth banisters of a staircase, their boltholes and rust marks undisguised and pleasing.

In the kitchen, Callahan tossed his cap onto a counter and cracked a half-dozen eggs into a pan. He made coffee and toast and scooped a pile of scrambled eggs onto a plate for himself. He set the meal out on a table on a deck behind the kitchen, where huge tree-ferns cast lacy

shadows and the sound of whip-birds came from the
dark, boughed archways of the rainforest.

Lori looked hungrily at the pile of toast. He pushed
it towards her. 'Help yourself.'

She tackled it with relish. 'I didn't have breakfast
either. And your colleague Tom didn't even offer me a
cup of coffee.'

'He must have liked you, then.'

Lori paused in enquiry, a marmalade-laden piece of
toast *en route* to her mouth, and he added, 'He makes
terrible coffee.'

She laughed, took a hearty bite and caught some
sliding marmalade in her palm. 'I doubt that. That he
liked me, I mean. I'm not the kind of woman that men
like on first acquaintance. Or even second or third,' she
said wryly.

'Why's that?'

'I have it on good authority that I'm too aggressive,
too humourless and not fashion-conscious enough.'

'What authority?'

'The Uncles, my cousins, my brother,' she said. 'Per-
sonally, I think they're skirting around the real reasons.'

'Which are?'

'I'm too smart, too ambitious and I make more money
than most men. Any one of those make a woman un-
likeable—all three together—' She raised one shoulder
in a shrug and licked the marmalade from her palm.

'Doesn't that bother you?'

'I know what I want in life,' she said. 'I discovered a
long time ago that I couldn't have it and please men as
well. I want my career more than I want to be liked by
men.'

She took some savage delight in putting the record
straight. Let Callahan and Tom be certain that she was
no forlorn spinster making her career a substitute for a
man because no one had 'taken' her. The strength of
her anger over it dismayed her. And what was she doing,

talking to a stranger like this? She really did need that island holiday. Island. The word failed to conjure up the inner peace she associated with it.

'What about lovers?' he said, prosaically scraping up the last of the scrambled egg. 'You must make some effort to please a lover.'

Lori felt the heat in her face but looked levelly at him and raised her cup. 'Any chance of more coffee?'

'You do like to call the tune, Ms Tate.' He leaned back with the expansiveness of the well-fed man. 'Any time the conversation reaches a point you don't like, you simply call a stop. Some might call you a domineering woman.'

'Some already have.'

'It would take a brave man to take you on.'

'They've said that too.'

Arms raised behind his head, eyes half closed, he regarded her lazily. A few coinspots of sunlight quivered through a fern frond and picked up highlights in his untidy dark hair. It looked glossy, tough and thick. Probably slippery to the touch. What did it look like loose? Just for a moment she imagined pulling it free from that band, seeing it fall forward to outline those hard cheekbones and the planes beneath. She looked into his dark blue eyes and her heart thudded, and she heard a sound like distant bells.

'But I've already been brave once today,' he said mockingly. 'Pity.'

The weird spell was broken. There was nothing here that couldn't be accounted for. She didn't like long hair on a man—any fantasies about it could be attributed to burn-out. The tinkling sounds were bell-birds, somewhere down in the rainforest. And lately her heart was always racing from too much caffeine.

Lori set her coffee-cup on the table. She eyed him frostily. 'I do not require a man to "take me on", as you so crudely put it. If it's a challenge you're after I would have thought your current financial position was stimulating enough for any man of action.'

That put an end to his sleepy, suggestive indolence. Callahan shot her a look of dislike and got to his feet to gather up plates and cups, piling them into the crook of one arm. His boots made clumping sounds across the kitchen floor and the crockery and cutlery clattered in an avalanche into the sink.

'Thanks for the reminder,' he said. 'For a while there I was starting to—I was forgetting that your last name was Tate. Let's get this over with,' he said tersely, and led the way outside to the car. 'It doesn't matter to me what you look at. To really see this place would take most of a day. I only demanded that a director come up here because I wanted the chance to make a Tate jump through hoops just once before you got your hands on my land.'

'I see,' she said. 'You like to play games.'

He let out a shout of laughter. 'Oh, that's good, coming from a Tate.' His sardonic humour continued in a series of muffled guffaws as they went to his car.

Starting to what? she thought. What had he been about to say? Starting to like you? She shrugged off a wistful feeling and reminded herself that her goals in life were simply not compatible with popularity.

They got it over with. After an hour and a half of jolting over private tracks and the unsealed road, he pulled up alongside her rental car again. Callahan removed his sunglasses and tossed them onto the shelf, impatiently crushing the newssheet with the crossword puzzle.

'Do you want the answer to twenty-eight across, or are you a purist puzzle addict who has to do it without help?' she said, indicating the faintly crackling paper.

He plucked out the sheet and looked up the clue. '"One who gives financial support,"' he said drily. 'Finance—your specialty.'

She wrinkled her nose. 'Finance doesn't feature much in my daily crossword puzzles. I think they are compiled by an ex-historian, and history is not my best subject.'

'You're a crossword fan?'

'Devoted.'

'A purist?'

'Absolutely. I have to figure them out all by myself.'

His expression was one of ironic amusement as he got out and walked around to open her door.

'And you're going on holiday all by yourself too, I take it?'

'All by myself,' she said crisply. 'Just the way I want it.'

'Well, Ms Tate,' he drawled, 'I reckon you're a woman who will always get what she wants.'

He got back in the car and drove the short distance to park in front of his office. He almost beat the slam of his car door onto the pavement. This was where she had come in.

Callahan didn't look back and she drove away, on holiday at last, thinking how much she had been looking forward to this moment. She felt rather flat. Absolutely alone. Paradise beckoned less brightly. 'You're a woman who will always get what she wants...'

Three days later, bare-breasted, her hair streaming wet over one shoulder, Lori sat on a rock surrounded by water, beguiled into idleness by the tempo of the tropics. Her paradise was not quite as she'd anticipated.

The island *was* uninhabited and her tent had been left behind as promised by a research team from a Queensland university. Fairlie had got permission for Lori to occupy the camp by offering Lori's services to the same university—a minor matter of daily inspecting rain gauges, recording rainfall and precipitation and watering some experimental plants in large tubs. Lori found the duties quite soothing.

But one thing Fairlie had forgotten to say was that the island had a twin, separated from it by a narrow strait of coral reef. She had also forgotten to say that the sister island was a tourist resort, swarming with people who sailed in catamarans and paddled in canoes and snorkeled tirelessly over the reef. And she hadn't said that at low tide the two islands were linked by coral and a sandbar, which brought some of the resort patrons over onto *her* island where they sunbaked and snorkeled until the tide turned.

At night Lori could look over at the resort glowing with lights among the coconut palms. Sometimes, when the wind changed, she heard dance music and the sound of laughter. It wasn't her scene—never had been. She'd never had time for dancing and parties, and now she rarely attended any but work-related functions, but at night, on her tranquil beach, she sometimes felt the wistfulness of an outsider and had to remind herself that it was what she wanted. 'You're a woman who will always get what she wants...'

Eyes narrowed against the sun, Lori watched a line of bubbles on the dazzling surface of the water. Here in this tiny cove, on the far side of the resort people, the sound of water and cicada buzz and bird-calls was uninterrupted by music or laughter, and the sands were innocent of castaway cans and empty sun oil bottles.

Out to sea, the waves would be breaking in white foam on the Great Barrier Reef that ran parallel to the coast for a thousand miles. Here, inside the wall of coral, the water lapped gently, raised now and then by a breeze into crestless swells. The sky was blue and immense over the layered colors of the water—translucent aqua, milky jade, ultramarine and purple over submerged reefs and rocks, and in the shallows, that elusive pale green-gold of crystal water over pristine sand.

The line of bubbles moved out from the glare of sun on water. Lori sat up a little as she saw the dark shape beneath the shattered surface glitter. She drew her feet up out of the water onto the rock. Shark? It was the conditioned response to that great Australian fear. But of course sharks didn't blow bubbles. The long, dark shape glided straight for her rock and she sat there, reluctant to dive into the water with an unidentified object.

The moments of sheer idiocy passed, and she saw that it was a diver just as he or she surfaced. He, she corrected as some fairly husky male shoulders broke through the water. The man looked up at her through his mask, blinked quickly several times and disappeared beneath the surface. He came up again and was gently shoved onto the rock by a swell. His air tank scraped it as he took a hold and removed his mouthpiece and mask.

Lori stared down at him and he stared at her. His dark blue eyes picked up the aqua tint of the sea. 'A Tate director,' he said, smiling so that the sun glinted on his wet lips. 'In the flesh.'

# CHAPTER TWO

HER heart pounded. 'Oh—Callahan. What are you doing here?' she said inanely. She crossed her arms over her naked upper body but his expression said, Too late.

'Lorelei.' He said it as both name and description of a woman, half-naked, sitting on a rock like a mermaid, with her breasts brazenly pointed at the sun. She had always disliked her full name, had always wished she had been given a sensible name like Laura. But Lorelei didn't sound too bad the way he said it, slow and deliberate, like the tasting of an old, rare wine.

She must have been too long in the sun. Her skin tingled with sunburn. Could she slide into the water without displaying too much? It wasn't possible. She had to uncross her arms to get off the rock without gashing herself on the sharp encrustations.

'It's a dilemma,' he said, noting her measuring glances.

'You could look the other way.'

'I don't think I can.'

'Why not?'

'No will-power,' he said sorrowfully. 'Sirens sap a man's will-power. They lure a man onto the rocks with their siren song and then—well, you know what the Lorelei did with their victims then, don't you?'

She winced, but kept her voice cool. 'Tore them to pieces, wasn't it?'

'A bit like the Tates, really,' he said drily. 'And you're a Tate *and* a Lorelei—a combination to strike terror into a man.'

'Shouldn't you be on your way, then?' she snapped.

'I'm feeling brave today.'

She manoeuvred herself into the water, well aware that he was getting an eyeful. 'I thought you'd seen all you wanted to see,' she reminded him with a baleful look.

'I thought I had too.' He watched her finally slip into the water, baring her all in the process. 'I believe they—er—*toyed* with their victims first,' he said, and his frank admiration piqued her and pleased her simultaneously. 'I wonder what song the sirens sang, Lorelei?' he added mockingly, for all the world like some ancient philosopher wrestling with an unanswerable question.

'I'll leave you to your idle speculation,' she said, and struck out towards the warm shallows.

Lori ran onto the beach, snatched up her towel to cover herself and turned to watch him wade ashore. Wetsuits were very unforgiving things—any little flaw in a human body that might be disguised by clothing was outlined ruthlessly in a wetsuit. His was plain and black and explicit, and it signalled that here was a man with virtually no physical flaws.

Lean, flat-stomached and long-legged, he looked, as most men did, as if nature had run out of ideas around the hip area. But he was as near perfect as a man could look in a wetsuit, walking duck-footed. If there was a flaw it could be the width of his shoulders, which created a slight imbalance, she thought, being academic and picky about it. What *was* he doing here, anyway?

He tipped his body sideways, unhooked his air tank and let it slide off one muscular arm. It was a strangely seductive movement, heightened by the fact that he didn't take his eyes off her. When the air tank was on the sand, he sat down and removed his flippers, then, standing again, dragged off the mask.

His wet hair appeared, caught into a pony tail. The Uncles and her conservative male cousins, who thought short back and sides was the signature of masculinity, would be mildly contemptuous. But his muscles flexed as he thrust a hand over his hair, squeezing water from it, and there was nothing remotely effete about the action. He wore a bulky diver's watch that heightened the square, powerful shape of that hand. *Toy* with him? It would take a more audacious Lorelei than her to do that.

Her instinct was to get away, but he might follow, and she wasn't about to reveal her camp to him. The occasional resort guest she met wandering around always assumed that she, too, was staying at the resort, and she didn't tell them otherwise. Oh yes, she thought, as that glinting sea-blue gaze met hers. He would follow her.

Her nerves relayed alarm at the thought, but an unexpected satisfaction too. His interest was intense, as real between them as the warmth of the sun in the air. The knowledge of it curled and languidly stole through her body, making her feel warm and receptive for all of five seconds.

'I arrived today. Didn't see you at lunch.'

So he assumed she was staying at the resort on the other island. Good. She shrugged. 'I don't eat at the restaurant.'

'Dieting? Haven't made friends? Still holidaying alone? Now there's a coincidence. So am I.'

Callahan. Staying at the resort just across the coral strait. Lori found herself at once wary and excited at the prospect.

'That *is* a coincidence—you coming here right now,' she said. And swimming right up to the very rock she sat upon.

'You think I might be pursuing you, Ms Tate?' He gave the mocking smile of a man who didn't need to go in hot pursuit of a woman. Why would he, with women like Justine practically throwing themselves at him? Anyway, how would he have known where she was going?

'Can you afford to go on holiday and leave your business in the—er—circumstances, Mr Callahan?' she enquired, and was rewarded with a faint dimming of that hands-on-hips confidence.

'I use "holidaying" in the broadest possible sense. I'm here to give a couple of lectures and I have time to mix in a little pleasure.' He smiled. 'We could do a few things together, on the principle of better the devil you know...' He flashed his teeth in a smile that crinkled up his eyes. Her heartbeat quickened—and her without a gram of caffeine all day.

'I told you; I like being alone.'

'So do I. But it's a drawback if you want to play tennis.'

'I don't want to play tennis.'

'Don't want to, or can't?'

'Please,' she said wryly, '*don't* offer to teach me, will you?'

'Ah,' he said, with a lazy smile. 'That's Plan A down the drain.'

'Aren't you getting hot in that wetsuit?'

'Aren't you going to ask about Plan B?'

She tied her shoelaces together, then hung the sand-shoes around her neck. Tossing her towel over one shoulder, she moved away along the sand. 'I'm going for a walk before I go back to the resort.'

'Don't be too long,' he told her. 'If the tide comes in you won't get across the strait without a boat.'

Exposing her breasts had made her look empty-headed, apparently. She widened her eyes, put a little Monroe breathlessness into her voice. 'Oh, I never would have thought of that. Goodbye.'

He came after her—just when she thought he'd got the message. It annoyed her and vaguely alarmed her too. This was a lonely spot, and she hardly knew the man after all. She turned her head away from him, showing a fierce interest in the casuarinas fringing the beach and the clumps of spiky plants that looked like cacti.

'They were supposed to be the start of a rope industry,' he said. She glanced at him, frowning, and he pointed at the spiky plants. 'Sisal,' he told her. 'A type of agave—Mexican, I think. The government, in its wisdom, planted sisal all around this island in the 1890s, thinking they might manufacture rope from it.'

Lori looked at the fleshy plants. 'Rope,' she said sceptically. 'Sure.'

He smiled. 'I'll show you.' He took a knife from the sheath at his waist. The blade caught the sun in a blinding flash and Lori was transfixed, her mouth dry, her heart thumping. She had seen the knife sheath, of course, but it hadn't registered. A lonely beach, a stranger with a knife. Without volition her hand went to her throat.

'For Pete's sake—you look ready to run a mile!' His voice was sharp with irritation.

'When a woman sees a man with a knife she thinks about running,' she retorted. 'You should approve. It's a survival instinct.'

He chewed that over. 'I guess I'm just used to being recognised as a good guy,' he said ruefully. 'Relax, Lorelei. I have no designs on your beautiful neck.' As he crouched down by the sisal spikes he looked up at her, eyes squinted against the sun. 'None that include a knife, anyway.'

Her hand clasped even more protectively around her neck. He saw a new kind of tension stiffen her muscles and his eyes narrowed before he turned away and hacked off one of the outer fleshy leaves in a casual, blood-curdling style. 'See.' He teased the cut end and drew up several coarse fibres. 'That's sisal hemp—when it's dried and cleaned. Used to make twine and rope. Sisal goes into upholstery and cheap brushes.'

'I'm so glad you told me that,' she said, earnestly polite. 'Now my holiday is complete.'

He laughed and tossed the cut sisal into the bush, then resheathed the knife. They walked on a little way into a tiny cove where a cluster of coconut palms spread stripes of grey-mauve shadow on the white sand. The shadow of his tall, muscular body overlapped hers on the sand. Disturbed, Lori watched the blending pattern and pondered ways to get rid of him before she headed back to her camp to think about this development.

'That was another government scheme,' he said.

And that was another of those bland, irresistible statements that demanded her attention. She looked around for clues and eventually, and with a certain reluctant respect for his methods, had to ask, 'What was?'

'Coconut palms.'

'They're everywhere around the islands here.'

'Not exactly native to the area, though. Some coconuts inevitably wash up on island shores and germinate, but by and large these were introduced from Indonesia. The government started a planting programme of coconut palms through the islands to provide food for shipwrecked sailors.'

She looked at him, suspecting a put-on. 'Shipwrecked sailors. Uh-huh.'

'Lots of shipwrecks along the reef in the old days— lots of shipwrecked sailors marooned in these islands.' His eyes crinkled with a smile that barely moved his lips.

'You're making it up.'

'Scout's honour.' He sketched a cross on the impressive contours of his chest. She wondered if he was hairy or smooth under that wetsuit, tried to remember if his army fatigues had hinted at a hairy chest. Lori dragged her eyes away.

'There was a plantation over on Brampton Island, and they used to transplant new trees to other islands from there.' He picked up a fallen coconut and weighed it in one hand. 'Some of those big palms over near the resort are a hundred years old now.'

'How do you know all this?'

'Survival is my business, remember?' he said, and took out his knife again. This time she didn't react. His eyes gleamed. 'Am I gaining ground?' he asked, but didn't appear to need an answer.

This was one very confident male, she thought. He had none of the obvious swagger she saw so frequently. His assurance was born of a genuine belief in himself, tested in deserts and jungles and on sheer rock-faces. Used to confident males, Lori suddenly realised how few she knew who had quite this air. It held a tremendous attraction—like seeing an original painting after galleries of glossy prints.

He inserted the knife-tip into a whorl at the base of the smooth brown nut, then wedged it between some ravelled palm roots, picked up a rock and rapped on the hilt. After several blows the coconut split and he prised it apart, revealing the inner fuzzy shell. Using the knife and his considerable muscle power, he bored a hole in the tough second husk.

Observing this exertion, she said wryly, 'And did the government plant knives for the sailors too?'

'Starvation makes a shipwrecked sailor very resourceful.'

His knife-tip went through into the core of the coconut. Lori leaned forward with childish eagerness. 'Is there any coconut milk? I've always wondered what it was like—not out of a can, I mean.'

Crouched down beside him on the sand, she watched him hack the fruit open to reveal a lining of coconut flesh. He cut out a creamy wedge and passed it to her on the tip of his knife. 'This is a ripe nut—flesh but no milk. If you had a thirst you'd pick a greener nut, because they have more liquid and less flesh.'

She took the offered piece of coconut and chewed it. It was dry, but the taste and texture were pleasant and familiar. 'I remember trying to open a coconut once when I was a kid. Not the outer husk, just the fuzzy round nut. It took me, my brother and two cousins hours to crack it. We used a hammer in the end.'

'Sounds like some good teamwork.'

'Oh, Carson and Ritchie and Mark were the team. I just hung around and was tolerated. I'd forgotten how we used to hang out together so much before...'

'Before what?'

'Before my mother died and I moved away and things changed—as they do.'

A wave of nostalgia hit her as she squatted there on the sand, leaning over to pick out some more of the dry fruit. He gave her the coconut, then went and picked up a greener nut and used his knife and strength on it. When the inner nut split, he quickly held one of the outer halves beneath to catch the small amount of clear liquid that ran out.

'Try it,' he said.

Gingerly she drank from the makeshift bowl. 'It's quite pleasant.'

'Shipwrecked sailors rate it higher than that.' He took the bowl back, tipped his head to drink the remaining milk, then wiped the back of his hand across his mouth.

His dark hair lay tangled over his forehead; his eyes were darkest blue and intent on her. A palm frond shadow lay across his face, jagged like shark's teeth. Lori felt a frisson. The breeze rattled the palms and the sea swelled along the shore and she stayed there, looking at him and the shifting shark teeth shadow, while thoughts she'd kept tamed a long time broke loose and ran wild.

His eyes glinted, as if he knew, and she tensed, but he said softly, 'The tree of life they call it—the coconut palm. Every part of it is useful. This stuff—' he rubbed at the fuzzy, fibrous inner nut '—is copra—that's the part that's pressed for coconut oil. Copra makes a natural mosquito repellent when it's burned. The outer shell makes good bowls and containers.

'These exposed roots—' he dug at the dry, spaghetti-like roots that sprang from the tree beside them '—will burn at high temperatures—high enough to fire clay. The leaves can be plaited into thatch for shelter; this mesh stuff around the leaf bases can sieve liquids. The growing tip is a delicacy, and the trunks make good support columns for a house.'

He stood up, and so did Lori. The odd spell was broken by his prosaic burst of information.

'And one palm tree has everything you need to make a canoe,' he finished. 'Sobering thought, isn't it? If we were shipwrecked here—you and I—we'd have everything we could want.'

'Shipwrecked . . . you and I . . . everything we could want.' She had been cutting down on coffee for three days now, but her heart pounded. Adrenaline instead of caffeine. Or something.

He smiled down at her. 'My name is Haze. Join me for dinner tonight?'

It had been nicely done. The generous back-off when she had been momentarily vulnerable, the soothing flow of trivia about palms and coconuts, then the firm re-iteration of his interest. I am civilised and patient, he was indicating. You can be safe with me. But that might depend on what you meant by 'safe'. Fairlie had told her to meet a terrific man and have some fun. And Lori felt tolerably sure that her cousin's artist wife would judge him a 'terrific man'.

'Haze?' she said, out of practice at this kind of thing and stalling for time. 'As in a haze around the moon, or a heat haze?'

His eyes flickered over her face. His teeth showed in a smile so vibrant it set her reeling. 'If you like,' he said softly, and she wished she hadn't used such evocative phrases.

'It's unusual. A showbiz kind of name. Is it one you made up yourself? Were you an amateur rock singer or something in your adolescence?'

'I can't even hold a tune.'

'Yes, but were you a rock singer?' she said drily.

He gave a shout of laughter. 'Nope. I was an outdoor kid. Horses, motorbikes, surfboards. Haze is the name my folks gave me. Adapted from Hayes, my mother's maiden name.'

Silence fell between them. His unanswered invitation lingered in the air. Lori glanced at him and met his eyes. 'I only packed shorts and T-shirts. I haven't got anything to wear,' she heard herself say.

'Come as you were,' he said, with a wolfish grin to remind her that she'd been almost naked a short time ago. But that had been the second time they'd met. She wondered what he would do if she turned up in the business suit that was presently crushed in the bottom of her tote bag.

'Will I call for you at your room or will we meet?'

'Oh, let's meet,' she said in rush, to avoid the subject of rooms and room numbers of which she had none. Her eyes closed briefly as she saw she had been manoeuvred by an expert into finally committing herself by making a choice from two alternatives, either of which suited him. She, who was familiar with all the tricks of negotiation.

They had run out of beach. A small rocky headland lay ahead, barring their way. 'I'll swim back,' he said, walking to the water. Looking over his shoulder, he said, 'What should I call you? You winced when I said Lorelei.'

No, she hadn't. She'd tingled all over at the sound of her burdensome name drawled in his smoky voice. But why hand him an automatic advantage? 'Call me Lori. Or Laura,' she called into the breeze. 'Yes—Laura.' Such a sensible name. She'd often wished she'd been named Laura.

'Tonight, Laura.' Haze lifted an arm in salute and waded through shallow water towards a channel of deep green.

She had meant to refuse his invitation, but instead had agreed. Haze Callahan was a man who would bear watching. Slavishly, she watched. The black of his wetsuit etched starkly against the glittering blues and greens. The long hair and the muscles, and the shoulders much too wide for the rest of his body. He dived into deep water and commenced a smooth, powerful crawl.

'I'm feeling brave today...' And it would be a brave man who took her on. He'd said that that day on his deck, while the bell-birds rang out their silver notes.

Lori abruptly turned her back, lest the man see her standing on the beach, gaping after him like an impressionable teenager. She had practically invited him to take her on. Today the phrase was as abrasive as ever, but in a challenging way. She was excited, more alive than she'd felt in ages.

Suddenly she laughed, the sound of it on the empty beach startling her. It was a long time since she had heard her own laughter.

# CHAPTER THREE

IT WAS the name that had clinched her madness, she thought hours later. And she had thought Laura such a sensible name. Whereas Lorelei Tate of Melbourne had long since decided that the most civilised of men were too much trouble, Laura of an uninhabited island was prepared to wade over reefs at low tide to meet a long-haired man who wielded a knife as casually as she herself used a pen.

Lorelei Tate had her clothes made for her in simple, classic designs in linens, pure wool and silk, but in the resort boutique Laura had bought an iridescent green dress with a strapless bodice and a short skirt with wired tiers that trembled with a life of their own. Lorelei was accustomed to elegant, understated hairstyles, but Laura had gone into the resort hairdresser and had her hair washed and blown dry into a flyaway wavy mass that swayed and shimmied like the wired dress.

Lorelei liked order and organization, a place for everything and everything in its place. Exactly five hours after leaving Haze Laura was in the resort's beach amenities block, awkwardly changing into her finery, putting on make-up by a very dim light.

Her fingernails, usually unpainted, flashed with tiger-ish gold polish as she stuffed her shorts, T-shirt and sandals into a bag. She could hardly take a beach-bag with her to dinner without raising questions, so she would have to stow the bag somewhere. Lorelei Tate was, for tonight at least, an itinerant.

Some time tonight, when the tide was out again, she had to change out of the green dress and wade across

41

the reef and get back to her camp in the jungle in the dark, with only her torch as guide.

Lori had a sudden snapshot of Haze, his eyes glinting with triumph and desire. No, she wouldn't *have* to go back to her camp. Haze would want her to spend the night with him, she was certain. Her breathing quickened. A soft bed and low lights and Haze's beautiful, top-heavy body close to hers. In her mind's eye she pictured herself naked in his arms, opening up for him. Her body ached. It had been such a long time...

She felt the heavy burden of guilt descend upon her. She wouldn't spend the night with him, of course. There was the business relationship between him and Tate's to think of. In her situation, she could not afford The Uncles and her cousins to be confronted at some future time by a man who'd bedded the only female director. She had to think of her future, her career.

No, there were a dozen good reasons why she wouldn't spend the night with him. Anyway, Haze Callahan wouldn't be the first charming, sexy man to turn out to be clumsy and heavy-handed—a grabber. He might be a dreadful sloppy kisser. He might have bad breath or body odour. He might have hair all over his chest *and* all over his back.

And Jekyll might turn into Hyde after a glass or two of wine. That intriguing meld of humour and sexiness might be just superb window-dressing and he might turn out to be an insensitive clod. Even dinner could be a mistake—there could be awkward silences and dire struggles for conversation.

Dutifully she summarised the potential for disaster and decided she would be better off to go back to the tent and practise the palm-weaving she'd started. The trek back to her camp in the jungle in the dark was probably the lesser of two dangerous ways she could spend the night. Or so Lorelei Tate concluded. Laura just wasn't listening.

\*    \*    \*

Haze was early, waiting for her. He wore a beige linen suit with a green, nearly black T-shirt beneath. There was an indefinable air about him, an ease about the way he stood that attracted attention. The suit jacket was a bit too crumpled, even for linen, and the T-shirt a mite too chest-hugging. But he looked extraordinarily good. A man who could rate nine out of ten in a wetsuit would probably look good in rags.

'Hello,' she said.

His hair was dark as jet and brushed smooth, tied back with a thin leather thong, and Lori felt again that odd mix of fascination and embarrassment. His eyebrows went up at her short, mad dress with its wired hems, at her mass of hair still shifting from the momentum of walking. She felt that everything about her was quivering—an unaccustomed sensation, though not unpleasant. It was galling how disappointed she was when he made no comment on how she looked.

They ordered dinner and drank champagne, and he didn't turn into Mr Hyde. He just got better and better. 'How long have you lived there in your rainforest house?' she asked.

'Six years, on and off. I go away for long periods sometimes—with trainees occasionally, but mostly on research trips. My mother or my sister sometimes moves in for a while to take care of the place while I'm away.'

'Where do you go?'

'The Simpson Desert, the Snowy Mountains, the Antarctic. I went to Turkey and the American west coast to research survival in earthquakes. I'll be doing some mountain work in Wales and Cumbria for a chapter in my next book.'

'I saw your books in your office. Surely you must make enough money from them to at least keep your house?'

'I couldn't survive on the income from books on survival,' he quipped.

'Why spend all that time researching them, then, if they're not worthwhile?'

'I didn't say they weren't worthwhile,' he said softly, after a count of four. 'Just that they don't make much profit.'

He actually looked sorry for her, as if he had decided that she only measured things in terms of cash profit because she was a Tate. 'Perhaps that's what's wrong with your business,' she pointed out, irritated by his moral superiority. 'Too many ventures that don't make much profit.'

'And maybe what's wrong with *yours*,' he drawled, 'is not enough things that are worthwhile.'

It cut sharply to some tender part of her that she hadn't properly acknowledged. Haze Callahan was a very disturbing man to be with, in more ways than one.

Their dinner came and their conversation continued through it. Lori came back time and again to the subject of his house and the magical stretch of land on which it was built.

'You seem unusually concerned about me losing my house,' he said.

'For a Tate, you mean?' she snapped.

'For someone who only met me a few days ago,' he said peaceably.

A few days? Lori stared at him, trying to think of a time when he hadn't been in her life, on her mind. 'It's just that I know how you must feel because I'm in a similar position,' she said. Unexpectedly she felt suddenly close to tears, as if this new emotional state brought on by Haze had loosened the control that had held her grief for Woody in check. She sought the language to hold it all at bay. 'I'm about to lose a property that means a great deal to me too,' she said.

He gave her a sardonic smile. 'Yes, it's tough losing a nice piece of real estate.'

Lori opened her mouth to explain that she'd had to reduce Woody's place to mere 'property' just to stop herself from bawling like a child at the idea of losing it, but the notion was soon gone. Even if she explained he probably wouldn't believe her. She was used to people thinking she was tough and cool and could take hard decisions without any emotional struggle. She even preferred it. There was, at least, a grudging respect for that in business. There was none for a woman who shed tears, or was sentimental.

The moment of tension passed. Music played. The buzz of people eating, talking, laughing was a steady undertone. He asked more about her childhood and she was plunged back into that curiously forgotten time, when she and Mark and her cousins had been kids. It fascinated her, loosened her tongue, and she talked about The Uncles and realised all over again that she was fond of the chauvinistic old tyrants.

'Uncle Errol's the real brain behind Tate's,' she told Haze. 'Clark fancies himself as a playboy, and his wife sports a new, desperate hairdo to counter every new girlfriend—as if she thinks it might tempt him to monogamy. His behavior is sending Aunt Cheryl quietly crazy and the old hypocrite has the nerve to say that *I'm* dangerous—' She pulled up short.

'Dangerous?' he prompted, eyes alert.

'To men,' she said, forcing herself to speak lightly. She looked him in the eyes and said, 'A man I was close to once years ago...died in an accident. He was hit by a car.'

Silence for the count of six. Lori noticed that he often paused like this. The people she knew rarely paused, because they feared that someone else might leap into the gap of precious seconds and take the initiative. Consequently there were few people who really listened.

'Bad luck,' Haze said, waiting.

She turned her wine glass in her hand, watching it. 'And two years after that I went to lunch with a man—not a personal date, you understand, it was a business lunch. He was fifty, overweight and stressed out of his mind. He had a heart attack at the table...' She glanced at Haze to see what he was making of all this. He nodded, waited.

'That's when I earned the X-names. The Hex. The Jinx. There are very few nice words with "X" in them, have you noticed?' she went on, talking too much. 'Uncle Errol called me the Siren—dangerous to men. Bad joke. On the other hand, my father died in a car crash only eighteen months after that tragic lunch, so maybe there's something in it after all.'

She managed a cool smile but she was aware of a renewal of that old nagging, superstitious fear. 'You're taking a big risk, having dinner with me. Are you sure you wouldn't rather skip dessert?'

'I'm used to taking risks,' he said, grinning. 'And I never, *ever* skip dessert.'

In fact he had two—with great relish. Crêpes Suzette followed by a mountainous slice of chocolate gateau. 'I have a very sweet tooth,' he admitted sheepishly.

He suspended his attack on the precipitous, cream-coated chocolate at the halfway mark. 'Buxom,' he said. 'Sexy.'

'What?'

He grinned. 'They're nice X-words.' His gaze flickered over the neckline of the green dress, which emphasised the upper curves of her breasts. 'Very nice indeed.'

She was caught unawares and flushed faintly, remembering that he knew exactly how buxom she was. Haze looked pleased that she could find no ready rejoinder.

'Mmm, excellent. Exceptional,' he said as he polished off the rest of the cake. 'Extraordinary.'

'Excessive,' she said drily, rising to the occasion this time. 'Not to mention toxic.'

For someone who had planned on solitude, Lori found it all very satisfactory. If there were silences between her and the man sitting across from her they were never awkward, and as for dire struggles for conversation, Lori couldn't remember a time when communicating had been so easy. He had wit and experience and a rough kind of charm unlike any she'd encountered. Lori felt herself smiling, heard herself laughing. If only he had short hair.

Short hair, long hair—she felt an urge to tell him that she was from the other island, to invite him to her camp.

'It would be wonderful to sleep out under the stars—' she said, leaning towards him at the table, imagining him with her in the moonlight. For him she would abandon her solitude. 'In the wilderness.'

He was suddenly the expert, smiling and indulgent. 'The tropics gone to your head, have they? You wouldn't sleep a wink, Laura, my sweet. The ground is hard, the wilderness is full of rustling, unseen things. It sounds romantic, but you can't imagine how dark it is at night once you venture beyond the lights of the resort.'

'You don't think I'd have the nerve to live out there alone?' she asked, eyes wide. She waved vaguely in the direction of her camp.

His eyes drifted over her bare shoulders and the vivid dress, came to rest on her fingernails, frosted gold in the hairdressing salon. 'You're not the type to rough it in the woods,' he said, with the supreme confidence of a man who knew his wilderness and his women.

She smiled, enjoying his monumental error, pleased to remain an enigma when he thought he was reading her like a book. 'Perhaps you're right,' she conceded, with a downward sweep of her eyelashes that should have alerted him. But men were dazzled by concession from a woman, and Haze was no exception. He smiled. He knew he was right. Arrogant devil. Buffered by her knowledge, Lori felt quite mellow in the face of such masculine certainty, quite relaxed. Which made a change.

They danced to a fast beat, circling around each other. Lori, unpractised at this kind of dancing, threw off her inhibitions and let herself go. Her hair swished to one side then the other. It felt good, earthy and natural, and she relished the freedom from pins and restraint. She wiggled her bare shoulders and felt the crazy skirt trembling around her as if it were alive—and she felt entirely alive herself, conscious of herself in a way she hadn't since she was seventeen. It was tremendous, childish fun. Until the music changed.

Haze caught her hand and pulled her slowly in to him. The first time they'd touched, she thought, feeling the sensation of it feather along her nerves. He circled her waist lightly, and her hands had to go somewhere so they went to his shoulders—which were, she reminded herself, quite out of proportion to the rest of him. Through his jacket she felt the ripple of muscle as he slid his hands across her back, moving her close so that their bodies touched fleetingly with each sway to the music.

His fingertips moved over her dress and her bare back with a curious, questing quality, as if he was testing the very substance of which she was made. The touch was light, full of finesse, counterpointed by the slight roughness of callused skin. Lori had a sensation of enormous energy held in check. She looked in his eyes and saw the intention there, but he held her loosely, so that she only had to step back to be free of him. Lori felt a rush of euphoria. She felt like a girl again, falling in love...

She swayed close and he breathed in a deep, sharp breath that expanded his chest, then pulled her hard against him as if she had said yes out loud. For a long moment he stared into her eyes, then bent to touch his mouth to her neck. Her eyes closed as the fierce sensation spread far from the point of contact. 'I want you, Laura-love,' he said in her ear.

Lori slipped her arm around his neck, felt the silken brush of his tied back hair, the warm, shifting muscles of his shoulders. He was a charismatic man who turned women's heads. He could have women galore and he wanted her. Laura-love. It sounded so good, so natural, said in that grainy voice of his. Laura. Yes, in future she always wanted to be known as Laura.

'Haze,' she whispered, turning so that her mouth moved against his jaw.

His blue eyes glittered. 'Shall we go?'

He caught her by the waist and almost marched her from the dance-floor. His impatience and the strength that swept her along checked her recklessness. She felt like a swimmer about to be engulfed in a tidal wave.

'Just give me five minutes—' She waved a hand in the direction of the amenities and, seizing her purse from the table, moved away, skirt quivering, the picture of a party girl off to do her hair, refresh her make-up, respray her perfume.

When she looked back she saw that Haze was seated at the table, smiling at a glass of champagne he held raised in front of him. As if he was celebrating.

The image stayed with her in the seclusion of the powder room. She was vaguely uneasy and put it down to the uncharacteristic speed with which she'd come to this point. From the mirror, a stranger looked back at her—flushed, tousled, bare-shouldered. An eager girl having last-minute doubts. But she wasn't a girl. She was a grown woman, and deep down she had surely never intended to wade back across the coral strait tonight?

Still, her stomach contracted. It was all too quick. He was too much. Lori had the weird notion that Haze might work on her as the potion had worked on Alice— shrinking her smaller and smaller until she vanished. This was sheer cowardice, she told herself. She couldn't face the idea of losing control. She was afraid of intimacy after banishing it so long from her life. Here was a near-perfect man—intelligent, civilised but with some tantalising rough edges, strong and capable, and with looks and a physique that made her weak at the knees. She would be mad to walk away from him.

Haze was no longer at the table. Lori looked around and saw him using a telephone at the bar. It irritated her. While she had wrestled with momentous doubts about the significance of spending the night with him he had made use of the time to make a phone call.

She had half expected to find him pacing the floor while he waited for her, or at least manfully curbing his impatience while he finished his champagne. If he could so calmly attend to other matters at a time like this, perhaps he didn't really want her badly at all. And she needed to have that, at least, if she were to break her rules of the past years.

Standing undecided at the table, Lori looked down at his empty champagne glass and saw a note beside it. It was torn from a phone message pad and had the name 'Callahan' scrawled across the top. 'Please phone Justine asap'.

Justine. Lori had all but decided she must have misunderstood about Justine. The lovely woman whose estranged husband was too bloody-minded to give her a divorce. The woman with the wayward son who needed a father. Lori had a mental snapshot of Justine and Haze in each other's arms, touching each other as if it were not the first time and would not be the last.

The message had come in just twenty minutes ago, and must have been handed to Haze while she'd been in the Ladies Room dithering about Alice in Wonderland. She looked over at him. Head down, he was hunched over the phone, creating a small, private world in which to talk to Justine. On the road that day, his body had formed a similar curve to protect the woman herself.

Lori waited, aware of a farcical element in all this. What would he say when he came back to the table? I've just been talking to Justine. Lovely woman. My place or yours? Or would he think twice about cheating on Justine and try to let Lori down lightly? Laura-love, on second thoughts this isn't such a good idea. She cringed at the idea of being the rejected party. Cringed, too, at the idea of spending the night with a man who would think of her as a little holiday fling on the side. Farcical? she thought, unable now to find anything funny about it.

A waiter came and cleared away the champagne glasses and the note. 'Would you like to order something else?' he asked.

'Nothing else,' Lori said, and quickly made her way outside. The green dress quivered and minced about her, shouting 'one-night stand' to anyone who cared to look. Shouting her loneliness and the susceptibility she thought she'd conquered when she was twenty.

Lori picked up speed, desperate to retrieve her beach-bag and change out of the iridescent dress that was telling tales on her. Island madness. That was it. So much sun-shine, simplicity and wholesomeness was bound to be too much for someone accustomed to great helpings of noise, pollution and the daily deviousness of the Tate Group of Companies.

'A near-perfect man!' she snorted under her breath as she made her way down to the beach, where the passage between the two islands glittered in the moonlight. The near-perfect man might not in the end have cheated on Justine, but he had certainly been planning to. He was no better than Uncle Clark, who cheated on Aunt Cheryl as if entitled to his peccadilloes. 'They don't mean any-thing,' Uncle Clark always told his wife. 'It's you I come home to.'

Lori shuddered, imagining Haze saying of her, Lorelei Tate, to Justine, She didn't mean anything to me.

She had more than an hour to wait until the tide re-ceded to let her pick her way across the coral strait. In the semi-darkness she changed into her shorts and T-shirt and stuffed the green dress into her bag with her heeled shoes. 'And good riddance, Laura,' she muttered.

The moon shed a soft ivory glow on the sand, the breeze rustled palm leaves, music drifted to her. She could be in his lovely, muscular, cheating arms now. Lori rifled through her beach-bag for the instruction booklet on palm-weaving she'd picked up in the resort shop that afternoon. Turning it towards the moonlight, she peered at the print.

For excellent results with palm-weaving one had to use the flexible green palm fronds, cut from the tree. That explained where she'd been going wrong. She had used dead leaves from fallen palm fronds. She could be in his bed now, lying next to that beautiful strong body, running her fingers through his hair, kissing his marvellous, plausible mouth.

'To make a small square mat take six palm fronds,' she read out loud. Lori had enviable powers of concentration, and she used them on the instructions for a small circular fruit bowl and a large floor mat.

At last the tide was on the turn. Lori looked up at the stars.

That night there was a haze around the moon.

# CHAPTER FOUR

HER experimental plaited palm strip was rather stiff but she tied it around her ankle. A few shells dangled from it and she admired her own rough handicraft with unexpected pleasure. Another band of plaited palm was bound around her head to hold back her hair, which felt wild and stiff with salt water again. She had plunged into the sea this morning and banished the last trace of yesterday's hairdo and last night's champagne.

Buckling her jeans belt low on her hips, over her bikini, she tied on the machete. She headed towards the shore, where palm trees grew. Here, the vegetation's growth had been shaped by the wind, and she found a bowed palm with a tangle of casuarina trunks alongside it that would give her access to the feathery green palm head.

Making heavy weather of it at first, she climbed the casuarina until she was high enough, then untied the wildly swinging machete and leaned out to hack a couple of lush green palm fronds off. They fell, rustling to earth, and she looped the machete to her belt and stayed there a while, looking. Lorikeets swooped past her in a flash of blue and green and crimson. A stray warm air current whipped the tip of a palm leaf into rhythmic motion. The lazy buzz of insects, the tropical heat of afternoon... the signature of paradise.

If only she hadn't met Callahan, it would have been perfect. Lori swished the machete and accidentally severed another frond. It fell a little way then stuck and remained there, even when she nudged it with the tip of the machete. Scowling, she began her descent. The man kept creeping into her mind, occupying her thoughts,

stirring up emotions and longings and she would not
allow it. She had better things to do than to wallow in
the details of a love affair that hadn't even eventuated
with a man who made phone calls to other women on
the way to bed with his latest conquest.

'Palm-weaving,' she said roundly, feeling it lacked a
certain something as an antidote to Haze. Nearer the
ground, between two forked branches, she reached down
a foot tentatively to a barely glimpsed lower branch and
paused to admire the effect of her anklet once more
before committing herself.

The branch below moved. She pulled her foot back
with a faint tinkle of shells. No branch at all, but an
arm. Shadows and sun shifted on a tanned, muscled arm
attached to a tanned, muscled shoulder. Her eyes fixed
on a small tattoo on the bicep.

A large hand pushed aside a bunch of casuarina
needles. Navy blue eyes looked up at her, roamed over
her legs to the anklet and up again to the bikini top that
was stretched to an imminent overspill as she leaned
forward in the tree. The machete swayed, making a low
swishing sound as it brushed against her thigh.

'It's the queen of the jungle,' he drawled.

'Oh. Hello,' she said weakly. Her heart was pounding
so hard that she felt certain the vibration would complete the bikini overspill that gravity threatened. In her
haste to get her feet on the ground she rammed her ankle
into a cleft, and her body was already too far forward
for balance. Haze held up his hand and she took it and
jumped the last metre. He staggered and fell backwards,
and as Lori sprawled over him he let out a short, sharp
exclamation and rolled so that she was pinned beneath
him.

Her hair was in her face, obscuring her vision, but all
her other senses were in fine working order. The weight
of his body pressed her down into the cushioning mat
of casuarina needles and sand. The rough texture of a

hairy chest and legs registered on her bare skin from neck to knee. The smoothness of his shoulders slipped like satin beneath the palms of her hands.

He swept the hair from her face and she looked up into his eyes. 'So, what happened?' he said, not letting her up. 'Did you get lost last night on your way to the little girls' room? Get cold feet as well as cold hands?'

'Let me up.'

She twisted beneath him, which was a bad mistake—for she was almost naked and so was he. His hands gripped her wrists as she shoved at him, and she felt with a slight sense of panic the full physical power of the man. He looked down at her, his anger already abating as he felt his superiority and control. His eyes flicked over her tangled hair and her face free of make-up, settled on her mouth. The world was full of breathy sounds, the susurration of palms, the shush of the sea.

'I want an explanation, lady,' he said softly. 'You left me sitting there like a prize idiot.'

She'd left him sitting there embracing the phone while he talked to Justine, but she wasn't going to tell him that. 'I left you sitting there drinking a toast to your conquest—as it turned out, it was a premature celebration!'

'A premature what?' he murmured, eyes glinting.

Lori coloured. Her breathing was shallow and fast. Her eyes wandered to the tattoo on his arm. As tattoos went it was modest—a four-leaf clover. But it made him seem suddenly tougher, more alien, a man whose life held nothing familiar to her.

Her hand pressed against his shoulder and her fingers caught in the band holding back his hair. It came loose and the hair fell forward, dark and glossy, giving him the fierce look of a Celtic warrior. Without volition she fingered some of the thick, glossy strands snared between her fingers. His eyes narrowed and he made a

small, guttural sound of approval as he lowered his head
and kissed her.

His lips were fierce then tender, demanding then deli-
cately persuasive, until she didn't know what to expect
and stopped wondering. Lori responded with all the pent-
up longing she'd felt for love itself these past years, and
for Haze himself these last few days.

It seemed to go on for ages this kiss, in endless variation, caress after caress. His big body pressed her down
into the soft matt of casuarina needles and sand and she
felt every ridge of muscle on him, the imprint of his
desire. She ran her hands over his arms, feeling the silken
rise and fall of biceps and the heat of his skin, grained
with sand. He was beautiful to touch, to hold.

Her hands circled over his back and up to his nape to
tangle in the long hair that had alternately intrigued and
repelled her. It didn't repel her now. The feel of it was
pure sensuality, and she gathered up handfuls of it and
tugged, taking pleasure from the small grunt he gave.
He pushed aside her hair and kissed her neck, her
shoulder, dabbing his tongue to her hot skin, leaving
coolness behind.

With a sudden athletic movement, he sat and pulled
her up from the ground into a close embrace. She felt
the fastening of her bikini top give and then he laid her
once more on the soft sand, naked to the waist, his big
hands a living garment covering her.

She heard her own groan of delight, reached for him
and laced her hands once again into his hair, dragging
him down with a wildness she'd never suspected in
herself, angling his head ready for her kiss. Vaguely she
heard a rustling sound overhead. Something hit her
sharply on the forehead and she cried out—in pain this
time.

'You OK?' Haze said huskily. 'There's a mark on
your forehead.'

He looked into her eyes and she could only hope he wouldn't guess at the schoolgirl embarrassment that paralysed her. She wanted to back right away from the fact of her response to him.

She sat up and snatched at her discarded bikini, held it to her chest. Palm-weaving had not, after all, been a bad choice as an antidote to Haze. It was the severed palm frond that had at last slipped down through the palm canopy and given her a much needed clout to the head.

Lori scrambled to her feet. Haze gave an ironic smile as she placed herself eloquently out of his reach then hastily put her top on.

'Want some help?' he mocked, but he kept his distance.

He felt around on the sand until he found the elastic from his hair, snapped it around his wrist. 'I enquired at the desk—the resort has no booking for Lorelei Tate. So where are you staying? One of the other islands? Have you got a boat?'

Lori fished out a scarf from the pocket of her shorts while she considered telling him about her camp. 'Something like that,' she said. 'Your leg is bleeding. You must have fallen on the machete point.'

'The machete point fell on me,' he retorted, inspecting the oozing cut on his thigh.

She folded the scarf lengthwise to present a clean surface and handed it to him. He tied it around his leg. Lori moved towards the beach, keen to draw him away from any tracks that might lead him to her camp.

'So why did you run out on me last night?' he asked, falling into step beside her. His shadow overlapped hers again. Or hers overlapped his. 'In view of recent events—' here, he ostentatiously brushed sand off his shoulders '—I can't think it was because you decided you didn't fancy me after all.'

She flushed. The man was not going to let her wiggle out of this gracefully. 'Well...' she said, as if she was seriously thinking of how to phrase her next statement. In fact her mind raced, trying to come up with something that would save her dignity without inflating his ego. It would have helped if she hadn't admired the man whose skill could save a life, if she hadn't seen his house and his frustration at losing it. In spite of everything she felt a certain kindred spirit with Haze Callahan.

'You got cold feet,' he said kindly—the sexually well-balanced male addressing a skittish female. 'That's OK. That's probably my fault. I might have come on a bit strong—practically dragging you off the dance-floor like a caveman.'

And then chatting to your woman-friend on the phone, Lori thought. 'That's true,' she said, gritting her teeth at the indulgent, teasing tone that made her a capricious little girl. This was intolerable.

'What are we going to do about it, Laura?' he said softly.

They walked on a short distance, then Lori halted. The words were out before she knew it. 'Haze—I've got a proposition for you,' she said in a businesslike tone.

He stopped and looked back at her with a narrow smile. 'I thought we already had the proposition on the agenda, but that's OK. I'm a man of today. I can take it if a woman propositions *me*.'

'It's quite clear that we have all the right circumstances for a holiday fling,' she said.

'The *circumstances* can't be exactly right,' he said with irony. 'You vanished just when we were about to fling.'

Lori refused to be distracted, finding strength in a return to her working manner. It was, after all, the one she was most at home with. 'And I'm sure that would be very—agreeable.'

He gave a hoot of laughter. 'Agreeable! Condemned with faint praise.'

'The thing is, a brief, meaningless affair would probably jeopardise any chance of us helping each other in a more lasting way.'

His eyes were mere slits now, and his fists were bunched on his hips. 'What the *hell* are you talking about?'

'I'm talking about not mixing business with pleasure,' she said, getting into her stride now. She set off along the beach again, and he put on some speed to come alongside. 'You are in danger of losing your business and your home. You need money, right? Well, I can arrange that.'

He grabbed her arm and jerked her to a standstill. He was in a fine temper, brows almost joined in the middle, his mouth a firm line. '*Money?*' He almost spat the word. 'You're talking about money?'

Lori tried to ignore that warm, hard grip, and went on as if she were presenting an argument to The Uncles. 'I'm suggesting that we strike a deal. A business deal. I will ensure that you have the funds to pay your tax and keep your business afloat, which means you won't have to sell your land and house and your business can continue unthreatened.'

His fingers tightened on her arm. 'A business deal with a Tate,' he sneered. 'And what do *you* want from this deal? Mortgages on everything I possess? My soul in hock to the Tates for ever?'

'Don't be silly,' she scoffed. 'Nothing so melodramatic.'

'What, then?'

'I want you to marry me.'

# CHAPTER FIVE

His handsome mouth fell open. 'What?' he said at last, into a water-washed silence.

'Just for a short time,' she assured him. 'Woody didn't stipulate that I had to *stay* married. I think a year would be long enough.'

'What?' he said again, louder.

'Well, all right—six months, then,' she conceded, tapping her index and middle finger on her brow while she mentally reviewed the terms of Woody's will. 'Yes, six months should be quite satisfactory.'

'Six months—' he roared, then his voice appeared to fail him.

Lori frowned. 'I really don't think I can come down from that—six months is probably the minimum time in which to establish a bona fide—'

'I don't want you to come down from six months,' he said between gritted teeth.

Lori elected to ignore the signs of his anger. He'd had the initiative taken away from him at the very moment when he'd thought it was his. Haze no doubt thought she should be stuttering and flustered so soon after his masterful lovemaking. Instead she was clear-headed and practical, and his ego was wounded.

Lori felt quite gleeful for a moment, until she recalled explicitly those hectic minutes on the sand, humiliatingly brought to an end by a falling branch instead of her own common sense and strength of mind. Hot sand beneath her, the heat of him on top of her, his bare skin smooth and moist . . . Lori took a deep breath and disciplined her thoughts, crushed her natural responses to

them. It was something she'd learned to do to survive
in the Tate organisation, and only lately had it failed
her.

The holiday had, after all, been good for her. Her
resolution was almost as good as new. Already she felt
a certain contempt for the teary-eyed wimp she'd been
when she came here. And as for Laura ... well, Laura
was simply a manifestation of all her accumulated frustration and repression. It was a good thing to get it out
of her system. Laura had been a kind of therapy. Now
Lori Tate was back to normal. And this was business,
she reminded herself. By far the safest kind of trans-
action with Haze Callahan.

'So—six months?' she said, when Haze failed to add
to his statement and stood there glaring at her. 'Are we
agreed?'

'Why?' he asked roughly. 'Why marriage?'

'You remember I told you I would be losing my home
too?'

He gave a jerk of his jaw which she took to be assent,
and she went on to explain about Woody and the will.
She kept it brief, and as she finished a cynical smile pulled
his mouth to one side.

'People like you can never get enough, can you?' he
sneered. 'You're already wealthy but you can't pass up
another fortune from your rich god-mama. It must be
a very choice piece of real estate for the dedicated Ms
Tate to consider marrying for it.'

She opened her mouth to tell him that Woody had not
been rich, that she had left no mansion packed with
valuables, but instead the accumulations of an inter-
esting life. But Haze looked contemptuous and she stub-
bornly refused to justify herself to this man taking such
a high moral tone. Besides, it helped in some obscure
way to keep her resolution firm, to leave intact his pre-
judices about her as a wealthy Tate.

'How long have you had this in mind?' Haze frowned as if something new had occurred to him. 'Did you set out to—*lure* me into this bloody ridiculous proposition?'

'Lure?' she repeated scornfully. 'It crossed your pal Tom's mind before it crossed mine, if you remember. But the idea didn't really take form until—just a little while ago.' Without realising, she made an awkward gesture back towards the site of that mad roll in the sand. Haze picked up on it, and she could see the rapid rebound of his confidence.

'So, you weren't pretending to be attracted to me?' he said, almost as if he was talking to himself.

For a split second Lori wondered if she could get away with saying yes, it had all been just a pretence. But she thought of the green dress, her laughter, the way she'd melted in his arms on the dance-floor, her white-hot passion back there beneath the palms. No man, however convinced that she was a mercenary woman, would believe that she'd been faking.

'Of course not. I told you—I was very tempted to— um—but it seemed foolish to waste a relationship that could be so useful to us both by having a mere fling. That's why I left last night after I'd—reconsidered. I've never found it wise to mix business with pleasure.'

'"Waste a relationship",' he repeated, looking at her with the kind of reluctant fascination one might have for a Hollywood science fiction monster. 'So, you simply stopped feeling attracted to me and began seeing me as a business partner instead?'

'Well—more or less.'

'Just like that.'

Lori half smiled. He wanted to hear her say that it had been a tremendous wrench to give him up as a potential lover. She felt a spurt of anger that it was only his ego that was hurt.

'I wouldn't say "just like that". Anything worthwhile takes discipline and effort,' she said blandly. 'And I think this alternative has more to offer both of us—don't you agree?'

Haze stared at her. 'You went without parties and dancing as a teenager to study, did without meaningful relationships in your twenties to concentrate on your career—is that your key to success, Ms Tate? Delaying self-gratification?'

Delaying? she thought, startled that she had told him so much last night under the influence of champagne. Denying, more like, in this case. It was far more depressing than anything she'd given up before. 'That seems to bother you,' she snapped. 'Men forever complain that women are weak and emotional and don't know what they want, but the moment they are faced with one who has the strength of mind to sacrifice a little momentary pleasure for higher rewards they carry on like spoiled boys!'

'Higher rewards!' he snarled. 'You mean money. I should be flattered, I suppose, that you were even tempted to make love to me. But there was no profit in that, so you went for the money. Cold hands, cold feet, cold heart.'

'But I can put you back in business,' she said flatly. 'If you're interested, I'll need to go over your books.'

'Lady, you can go to hell,' he said between his teeth. 'I wouldn't marry you to save my whole family from being thrown on the streets. I'd rather handcuff myself to an iceberg! Keep looking for a husband, honey. I'd sooner be down to my last cent than get married to a woman like you!' He jabbed an index finger at her.

'Aren't you protesting too much, Haze? You *know* this is a good idea. It's not as if it will make any difference to your private life, because Justine can't get a divorce anyway.'

His eyes narrowed. 'Justine? How does Justine come into this?'

'For heaven's sake, do you think I'm blind? You and Justine practically burst into flame on the road that day, and that was when she was worried sick about her son! You're not going to tell me that there has never been anything between you!' Just for a moment Lori hoped he might say just that.

'No,' he said thoughtfully, after a count of six. 'I'm not going to tell you that.'

Being proved right was usually more satisfying. The man hadn't even bothered to dress it up—he and Justine had something going and Lori Tate had been a passing challenge, less memorable than a good climb on a rock-face. 'Well, then. Our deal would leave you free to carry on just as before where Justine is concerned. I'm sure it won't bother her that you're married if you explain that it's only a technicality.'

His gaze was steady, his expression inscrutable.

'Of course, if her husband rethinks a divorce, you only have to let me know and we can arrange an annulment to free you.'

'I could fax you,' he said sardonically. 'Tax. Fax. You're right about those X-words.'

'And, as I said, we could bring it to a logical conclusion anyway after six months.' Lori felt she'd covered every point. She felt good while she kept her mind on this level. 'You must admit, it is an excellent plan,' she said, prompted into detached admiration for the scheme. 'There's an almost architectural symmetry to it, don't you think?'

'Just what I was thinking. Architectural symmetry,' he said drily.

'We both get to keep what we value and neither of us has to make any heart-wrenching changes or give up our freedom or our personal goals. Nothing like real marriage.'

'Some people think you gain more than you give up in real marriage.'

'Yes.' Lori wrinkled her nose. 'Men, mostly.'

Something had altered. Lori couldn't quite figure out what. He was still angry—furious, even. But there was a calculating gleam in his eyes that might mean he was reconsidering the proposition. Certainly he was reconsidering *her*, scrutinising her skimpy bikini top and shorts with a crude familiarity that made her grateful she'd chosen business rather than pleasure.

Eyes still on her, he took the elastic from his wrist and flicked his head back once, gathered up his hair in one hand and snapped on the band with a couple of deft twists. His arm muscles, lightly sheened in the brilliant light, rippled with each tiny move. He made the small task a definitive masculine thing. Lori chided herself for thinking it could ever be any different when he did it.

While her eyes lingered on his neck he moved in speedily, wrapped an arm around her waist and yanked her hard against him. In the same continuous flow of movement he tilted her head back and kissed her hard on the mouth. Had he left it at that, she might not have sunk back into regret. But he had to kiss her on the neck—on the precise spot he had evidently identified from her own sigh of pleasure not so long ago. And he had to kiss her mouth again—with lingering softness instead of that harsh authority that would have made a business relationship a joyful alternative.

Lori felt his lovely shoulders under her palms, his skin warm and moist, and smelled the scent of him and kissed him back. He released her as abruptly as he'd reeled her in. Grimly satisfied, he eyed her as she blinked and touched her tongue to her lower lip.

'The pleasure wouldn't have been *momentary*,' he said.

Lori watched him stride away, leaving formless footprints in the soft sand. She hadn't lost her head in a silly affair with a man otherwise engaged and he'd rejected her proposition. 'Thank God,' she said out loud.

He would soon be back where he belonged, surviving the knocks, because that was what he did. And soon she would be back where she belonged, surviving the knocks because anything else was unthinkable. In Melbourne, he would be just another name on another file. She wouldn't see Haze Callahan again.

He was waiting by the pier when the charter boat took her back at the end of her holiday. Lori didn't notice him until the last minute because she was looking back to where she'd been, which seemed, in spite of everything, less lonely than where she was going. In a week—less—she would feel as if she'd dreamed the island and Haze Callahan. Haze. Already it sounded like the name of an imaginary man. Lori gave a humorless chuckle. She was too old for imaginary playmates.

Then she turned as the boat slowed in to the pier, and saw him leaning on a jetty rail, his eyes shaded by his ridiculous cap. He wore jeans and the same dark green, almost black T-shirt that he'd worn at the resort. He was solid, real, this man she'd dreamed. Lori's heartbeat quickened.

The charter skipper put her luggage ashore and Haze picked it up. 'I will,' he said.

'You—will what?'

'I will marry you.'

Lori stared. 'You said no before.'

'I'm more desperate than I thought.'

'You said you wouldn't do it even if all your family were thrown on the streets,' she reminded him, driven by a thin thread of panic. 'You'd rather be handcuffed to an iceberg.'

Carrying the bags, he led the way along the pier. 'All true. But I need the money,' he said flatly. 'You were right—it's a damned good deal. Besides—'

Never had she been so right, so often—and felt so bad about it. 'Besides, what?'

Callahan slanted a smoky, malicious look at her. 'Icebergs eventually melt.'

And then he'd be handcuffed to thin air. Free, in other words. She supposed that was what he meant, but her thoughts were too chaotic to follow the logic of his metaphor.

'I have to get a taxi to the airport,' she told him unsteadily as she saw that they were heading towards his parked four-wheel-drive. It must have been raining again in the hinterland. The bulky vehicle was splashed with mud.

'You'll have to cancel your flight today.' Haze tossed her luggage in the back of the car. 'I've booked you a room at a hotel. The wedding will be on Saturday. Two o'clock. You have no objection to an afternoon wedding?' he asked solicitously.

Lori dragged in a deep breath. She felt she was being swept along by some powerful force. But the plan was hers, of course.

'How did you know when I'd be arriving on the mainland?'

'Saw the boat charter name on that brochure in your attaché case,' he said easily. 'As it happens, I know the guy who runs it, so—' He shrugged one big shoulder. The man would be a riot in France.

'So much for client confidentiality,' she snapped, then, brushing away the cobwebs of living in island time, where naming days was not necessary, 'Saturday? But that's—tomorrow! What about the licence?'

'Get in,' he said, yanking open the passenger door. 'A mere formality—the papers are waiting for the bride's signature. We'll drop by and fix that now.'

Haze made an impatient shoo-in gesture as she hesitated by the open door. 'Come on. I've done all the legwork on your architecturally symmetrical plan. The least you can do is show a little enthusiasm. Think of that nice bit of real estate in Melbourne—yours for the price of a marriage certificate.'

But, oddly enough, she wasn't thinking of Woody's place at all as she got into the vehicle. She was thinking that it would be very easy to lose sight of every sensible principle she'd lived by. There was a glitter of resentment and unresolved challenge in his eyes that told her he intended to get an outcome from this peculiar relationship of theirs. And if it wasn't a business outcome, it would be one of pleasure.

As the vehicle hurtled past holiday villages nestled in palms and hibiscus Lori decided that she wouldn't stand a chance if he was determined on the latter. Just seeing him again had her blood racing. It was quite clear that she had to marry him if she wanted to keep him at arm's length. There seemed a flaw in that somewhere, but Lori re-examined it and couldn't find it.

They stopped briefly at a bank and Lori signed some papers which were witnessed by a justice of the peace. Haze folded them. 'I'll attend to these,' he said.

Lori was uneasy. As they returned to the car she felt as if she had just done something momentous. Ridiculous, of course. A mere formality. She'd signed far more significant documents in her work—contracts for millions of dollars. Even so. She looked up at Haze as he stood, holding open the passenger door for her. He certainly seemed very pleased, very relaxed. Annoyingly so.

'You never did tell me the answer to number twenty-eight down,' he said, grinning.

Well, he had certainly adjusted quickly to the advantages of a marriage of convenience. All that smouldering resentment at the fact that they'd failed to become lovers seemed to have vanished. Lori got in the car, angry with him and astonished at her own capriciousness. This was the point of the whole thing, wasn't it?

'Number twenty-eight down,' he said again, leaning into the cabin, his hands on the roof-edge so that his arms were raised and his shoulders extended. The dark green T-shirt strained at the seams, faithfully outlining his pectoral muscles and emphasising the powerful column of his neck. She swallowed and rummaged in her bag for sunglasses. Maybe dark lenses would dim this display that could only remind her of pleasure, not business.

'"One who gives financial support",' he quoted. 'I never did work out that clue.'

'Oh. It's angel,' she said, looking past him at the perfectly fanned foliage of a travellers' palm. 'Mostly used in showbusiness. The Uncles were angels once. They financially backed a musical spoof on *Cats* called *Rats*.'

'Never heard of it.'

She wrinkled her nose. 'It bombed after two weeks. The Uncles decided they were no angels. Now they stick to construction and development.'

Haze laughed heartily as he slammed the door shut. Everything was fine for him. He hadn't lost a lover, he'd gained an angel. And he had Justine too. Lori gritted her teeth, wondering how she'd been so stupid as to come up with a plan where *he* got the lion's share of the goodies. The only thing *she* was getting was Woody's place. She blinked behind her sun lenses. The *only* thing? What was she saying? Woody's place as a home, with her career and her independence undiminished—these were the things she valued above everything.

Absently, Lori's eyes followed a passing station sedan with nodding fishing rods lashed to its roof. She tried to work up some enthusiasm about wiping the smirk off Mark's face, but her mood remained curiously flat. Of course, all they had at present was paperwork, and paperwork could be torn up.

'I've arranged for the celebrant to marry us at my place,' Haze said, breaking into her reverie. 'A registry office is out, I'm afraid. I have family who have expectations about things like weddings,' he said.

'You're not inviting your family?' she said, vaguely aware that she had finally committed herself with this question. A chill passed over her heated skin.

'Only one or two.' His tone was mild and unconcerned. 'Unlike you, I care what my family think. They've waited a long time for my wedding and they'd never forgive me if the family weren't at least represented.'

'I wish you'd stop saying *wedding*,' she snapped. 'This is not a *wedding*. It's a business deal that just happens to require a simple marriage ceremony.'

'*We* know that. But for my family's sake I don't want it to look like a board investiture,' he said drily.

'You'll be living here and I'll be in Melbourne, so sooner or later they're going to realise it isn't a proper marriage.'

'I'll worry about that sooner or later,' he said smoothly, and, slowing the vehicle, he reached over and hauled a large wrapped parcel from the back and dumped it in her lap. 'A wedding present, darling,' he said.

It contained copies of his company books and financial dealings. Lori suddenly had an aversion to the idea of going through them. 'Ring me when you've had a chance to read them,' he said briskly. 'I'll be at home tonight.'

With or without Justine? she wondered. How had the redhead reacted to the news of his forthcoming marriage? She bit her lip to stop herself mentioning the woman's name.

'We'll need to have a few refreshments for the family representatives—for the sake of appearances,' Haze went on.

'Refreshments?' She shook her head. 'I don't want to hang about afterwards. I have to get back to work.'

'My impatient bride,' he drawled. 'What will you wear?'

Her snort of exasperation only amused him.

'That's OK,' he said as he drove into the hotel fore-court. 'It's bad luck for the groom to know what the bride will be wearing.'

She wore the suit and blouse she'd travelled in from Melbourne, suitably cleaned and pressed at the hotel. 'Something new,' she muttered with grim humour as she pulled on brand-new tights bought to replace her others—predictably laddered. Her hands were shaking. Anyone would think she truly was a bride. But then, weddings made everyone nervous, didn't they? But it wasn't a *wedding*, she amended. Just a short, meaning-less ceremony that would profit them both.

Haze sent a car. She had expected his mud-spattered four-wheel-drive chauffeured by Tom, but instead an orchid-coloured limousine with ribbons and a smirking bride-doll on its bonnet collected her and her luggage from the hotel. Lori eyed the decorations with resig-nation. Haze's little joke. The grizzled driver was a friend of the Callahan family, he told her, looking quite nos-talgic at her tailored suit and blouse.

'My old mum got married in an outfit like that,' he told her. 'During the war.'

So she looked like a no-frills war-bride. What did that matter? This was a business arrangement, pure and simple. Less personal, even, than a marriage of con-venience. She had never been the type to hanker for a wedding at all, let alone white lace and veils and big bouquets of fragrant flowers...

When she arrived Haze handed her out of the car and looked the suit over. 'Dressed for business, I see,' he said drily.

He wore a dark suit that made the most of his height and breadth of shoulder. His tie was slightly off centre and his collar button appeared to be undone, but the formality of the clothes made him a stranger again.

Lori hesitated by the open door of the car, suddenly apprehensive about this symmetrical scheme of hers. She shouldn't be here. Shouldn't be doing this. Didn't know him well enough to trust him as a partner. It wouldn't work. With a hysterical laugh that she only just suppressed, Lori thought that these must be the things that real brides worried about at the last minute.

The bride-doll simpered at her, big blue eyes wide and blank. Lori opened her mouth to say that this was a mistake, turned her body slightly to get back in the pale pink limousine, but Haze had a powerful hold on her and swung her inexorably round and slammed the door shut. To have and to hold, from this day forward... The same hysterical laugh threatened to burst forth.

Two women wearing emphatic hats approached them. The elder of the two looked intently at Lori's face and gave what seemed like a nod of approval before she moved close and put her arms around her. Lori was enveloped in a silky embrace, her nostrils assailed by the soft, sweet fragrance of face powder that she hadn't smelled since she was a child.

'My dear, I'm Haze's mother. Call me Meg.' She held Lori by the shoulders and eyed Lori's suit and blouse in commiseration. 'Oh, you poor girl!' she exclaimed. She rounded on her son, slapped his muscular arm with the backs of her fingers. 'Couldn't you have given her time to buy a dress to be married in?'

Haze grinned down at his mother. 'I told you, Mum. I couldn't wait. She might have slipped through my fingers.' His arm tightened around Lori's waist, cinching her in close to his side in a parody of affection. 'My angel,' he said, looking deep in her eyes.

'Well, my dear, he's altogether too sure of himself in my opinion. So if you have him feeling he has to try harder, I take my hat off to you!'

Lori's gaze went involuntarily to the woman's blue hat with its tiny veil and long feather quill. Meg Callahan kissed Lori soundly on both cheeks, and the feather stroked Lori's chin twice. The fragrance of face powder brought back childish memories of goodnight kisses and silly songs sung in her mother's voice. She swallowed hard, dismayed by this rush of memory.

'I think you should know, Mrs Callahan, why this is all so sudden—' she began hardily.

Haze squeezed her so hard she could scarcely breathe. 'Now, darling—you'll have my mother thinking you're pregnant,' he said, and directed such a smoking, heavy-lidded look at her that she was sure anyone watching would have believed it was entirely possible. Half embarrassed, half angry, she flushed, and he dropped an indulgent little kiss on her nose.

Meg fondly patted her shoulder. 'I suppose it is sudden, but Haze always knows what he's doing. We're a close family, but we don't ask questions when we're getting the red light signal. As far as we're concerned, you're one of us from now on.' Her shrewd gaze flicked between Lori and her son, then she nodded, and the long blue feather provided an exclamation point.

'Now—we'll have to do something about this suit,' she said, flicking a finger at the lapel of Lori's jacket. She disappeared, leaving the younger woman to eye Lori with warm curiosity.

'My sister, Jackie Duncan,' Haze said. 'Jackie organised the refreshments at short notice.'

Lori smiled stiffly, irritated that he was manipulating her good manners. 'Oh—er—thanks very much.'

Jackie embraced her. 'You look nervous. I'm not surprised. Metting Haze's family on the very day you join it. You'll feel more relaxed once the ceremony starts. I know I did. My husband couldn't come—Robert's a pilot for an air freight company and couldn't change his schedule at such short notice. Have you met Amanda yet? She's around somewhere—oh, excuse me, the punch bowl's arrived...'

More people arrived with the punch bowl. Car doors slammed. Music wafted out of the house. A man wandered around, laden down with photographic equipment.

'A photographer,' Lori said between clenched teeth. 'You didn't say anything about a photographer.'

'Oh, that's only Gary—he does the photographs for my manuals. You saw some of his work in the office. He's a friend from way back. No way could I keep Gary away.'

Tom was there too, his thinning hair carefully spread over a freckled scalp. Lori heard him telling someone that he'd known this would happen the minute he saw her and Haze together. 'Chemistry, know what I mean?' he said, with the superior air of one who had been there at the beginning. 'Oh, yes, doesn't surprise me one little bit.'

She refused to meet Haze's eyes as this carried clearly to them. Chemistry? What rubbish, There hadn't been anything of the kind—not immediately, anyway. The old hypocrite seemed to have forgotten that the only good thing he'd had to say about Lori was that she had plenty of money and her legs weren't bad.

'One or two people, you said,' she reminded Haze in a furious whisper. 'You've invited the whole damned district.'

'You know how it is—you invite one, then you know someone else will be offended if they don't get an invitation, so—' He shrugged his big shoulders in mock penitence. His shirt collar parted and he made an unsuccessful attempt to refasten the button, yanking the tie casually into place. It remained slightly off centre.

'Huh! I wouldn't be surprised if Justine turns up,' she snapped.

He smiled seraphically down at her. 'No. Justine said she couldn't face seeing me get married.'

Lori felt the sharp sting of jealousy. This was business, she reminded herself. Even if there had been no Justine, it would have to be that way. A man in her life—truly in her life—would be too troublesome, too exhausting. Too distracting. 'For heaven's sake—I know you want to convince your family, but must you look so—so—?'

'Lovesick?' he said, still wearing that warm expression that was, she reminded herself, just a smokescreen. 'They expect it—they know I've never fallen this hard before.'

'How would they know that?'

'I've never wanted to marry anyone before.'

Lori stared dizzily at him. He looked so—loving. So sincere. What a superb actor he was. 'You mean you've never *appeared* to want to marry anyone before,' she said briskly. 'Don't they know about Justine?'

He grinned. 'I don't tell my mummy every little thing,' he said, apparently unperturbed about the deception he was pulling on his mother, or the casual way he was talking about the love of his life as if it was some tawdry affair.

Lori was unexpectedly furious with him, and disappointed. But why was she surprised? She had grown up in a family full of men who made use of the sexual double standard one way or another. It was all making her feel very edgy. She needed to calm herself, *do* something to restore some sense of order in this unexpected chaos. Her gaze lit on his untidy shirt collar, and to his surprise she set to, neatening it.

'Your sister mentioned someone called Amanda,' she said, struggling with his collar button. The buttonhole was stiff because the shirt was brand-new.

'She's your bridesmaid, or attendant—or whatever you call it,' Haze said.

'What?' Lori glared at him. 'You've organised a *bridesmaid* for me? A bridesmaid is supposed to be a close friend of the bride. I don't want some strange woman for my bridesmaid!'

Lori bit her lip. What was she saying? She didn't want a bridesmaid at all. She straightened his tie with a vicious little jerk and picked some lint off one broad shoulder. The suit looked brand-new too. For some reason that bothered her.

'You're so damned insensitive, it's probably one of your old girlfriends! Well, this isn't a wedding and I don't *want* a bridesmaid—ouch!'

Her arm was squeezed hard as Haze swung her around to face a small girl wearing a long blue dress and a straw hat bedecked with daisies and forget-me-nots. 'Laura, this is Amanda. Jackie's daughter. My niece.'

Lori looked down into anxious hazel eyes fringed with pale lashes. The little girl was covered in freckles. 'Lori,' she said weakly.

'Auntie Lori,' said Haze.

'I'm not a bridesmaid,' the child said, with an air of disassociating herself from an unpleasant species. 'I'm a flower-girl.'

Lori forced the frown from her face. It didn't seem civilised to let her own annoyance upset a child. 'Oh—um—a flower-girl. That's different.'

'I've never been a flower-girl before, Auntie Lori,' Amanda said uncertainly.

*Auntie Lori.* They were closing around her, these Callahans. Lori remembered her lovely symmetrical plan that meant no heart-wrenching changes, no sacrifice, no involvement, and was furious that Haze had complicated matters by bringing all these nice people here to deceive them.

If only they had given her a lukewarm welcome, treated her as an interloper, she could have walked out on the whole plan. But she couldn't now. Trapped by niceness. Lori didn't have the heart to tell a child of five or six that this celebration was a mockery and that she didn't want a flower-girl. Her pinch-penny smile of acceptance was rewarded with a generous affection that made Lori feel like a miser.

'I'm sure you'll be very good at it,' she said in final surrender. 'What a lovely dress.'

The little girl tucked her hand into Lori's and appointed herself guide in this foreign land of people who kissed and hugged strangers as if they belonged.

She didn't have the heart, either, to say no to the gauzy cream scarf—'something borrowed'—that Meg draped over the severe lapels of her suit, or to refuse the prayer book that Jackie pressed in her hand. 'Something old *and* something blue,' Jackie said, and went on with a gurgle of laughter, 'The bookmark is the blue part, of course.'

Nor did she have the heart to reject the bouquet of tuberoses, orchids and miniature pink roses that Amanda proudly handed her as they stood with the celebrant on Haze's back deck.

She must have said all that was necessary as she stood beside Haze in the lacy shadows of the tree-ferns while bell-birds made their crystal-clear calls in the rainforest below, for suddenly she heard the celebrant say, with an air of finality, '...man and wife.'

Lori looked at Haze then, conscious of a superstitious fear that she had meddled with something she shouldn't have in this simple ceremony with its time-honoured phrases. Eyes wide, she was faintly surprised to see that Haze looked sober, even troubled, as if he might be thinking the same. But it lasted only an instant. He accorded his usual six-second pause before he responded to repeated cries of 'Kiss the bride', and then he kissed her.

If he had wanted to convince his family that all was well with this whirlwind marriage, the kiss would have lulled any fears. He caught her close in his arms, tender and possessive and sheltering, and kissed her so that even

Lori could almost believe she was the woman he had waited for all his life.

When he stopped she stood numbly in the curve of his arm, almost engulfed in a wave of emotion. Her thumb stroked at the foreign gold band on her third finger. I wish it were all true, she thought. The ceremony and the time-honoured phrases and the promises...

The enormity of it stiffened her backbone. She was getting carried away with the ritual and the emotions of Haze's female-dominated family—intoxicated with the sunshine and the lush green beauty of the forest and the heart-rending beauty of the bell-birds' calls. And the heavy scent of the tuberoses was affecting her brain.

Mercifully, there were no speeches afterwards, only a party-like atmosphere as people ate and drank and Gary took photographs.

Showered by confetti, Lori and Haze drove away at last in the four-wheel-drive—which some wags had decorated with what looked like shaving cream, streamers, climbing ropes and old hiking boots. The family thought they were heading off for a honeymoon at some secret destination. In fact, they would go their separate ways at the airport.

Before they turned onto the main road, Haze stopped and removed the boots and streamers. Lori got out to help erase the scrawled messages from the body of the car, but whatever had been used left a silvery trail on the paintwork, as if a giant snail had laboriously spelled out the words 'Just Married'. She rubbed hard at the marks, which seemed permanently etched on the surface. 'What an idiotic tradition this is,' she said crossly, panting with her efforts. 'Sheer vandalism!'

She looked around to find Haze watching her. 'You can't scrub some things out so easily, Laura-love. If you're having regrets about this excellent plan of yours, it's too late. We are married and we'll stay that way until we do something about it.'

Till death us do part... She scowled, shaken by a superstitious foreboding. 'Don't psychoanalyse me! I'm simply trying to rescue your paintwork, that's all. And don't call me Laura!'

'You asked me to call you Laura on the island,' he pointed out.

'Yes, well, that's where I want to leave Laura,' she muttered, straightening up from her fruitless task to toss the cleaning rag at him. 'Call me Lori,' she said.

'Lori Callahan,' he said experimentally. 'Doesn't sound too bad.'

'Lori *Tate*,' she snapped, shaken by the sound of his name with hers. 'I didn't marry you for your name—just a marriage certificate.'

His eyes narrowed. 'Well, you've got that,' he said, his voice turning harsh. 'Just make sure I get my part of the deal.'

'Your financial difficulties will be resolved just as soon as I can organise the finance, I promise you,' she said stiffly.

'Should I sleep easy at nights—my future relying on a promise? After all, you've already got what *you* want.'

She smiled coldly. 'It wasn't *me* who set the date. And you can hardly blame me if I go along with something that favours me, can you? Rule of survival in business: never complete your part of a bargain until the other person is committed. You shouldn't have rushed into the marriage ceremony until you had a financial deal in writing. I can't imagine why you did.'

His eyes glittered. 'Well, ma'am, I guess I'm just a fool when it comes to big business.' He shoved the boots, ropes, streamers and cleaning rags in the back of the car. 'I'll just have to trust you now.'

He turned in time to see her slide the wedding ring from her finger. She held the gold band out to him. It looked brand-new too. 'You should be able to return this,' she said. 'Get a refund.'

His nostrils flared. 'Keep it,' he growled, and he looked so blazingly angry that she took a step back. Male pride, she supposed, at her suggestion that he could use the money. She slipped it in her jacket pocket in a heavily brooding silence.

Lori looked him in the eye. 'You've kept your part of the bargain and I will keep mine—so you *can* sleep easy. We have a deal. I always keep my promises.'

The car door clanged shut. Haze leaned on it. 'You made a few this afternoon,' he said softly. 'Are you planning to keep them?'

To have and to hold from this day forward...love, honour and keep...keeping only unto to him...Lori's mouth opened and shut.

He gave a wry smile. 'I rest my case.'

She flew back to Melbourne, wondering just how she was going to break the news. What did you do on your holiday? Oh, swam, snorkeled, learned palm-weaving. Got married. *I'm married to the man.*

A small laugh escaped her and the passenger in the neighbouring seat cast a wary look in her direction. Lori rested her head and gazed down at the earth. She should be literally on top of the world after a holiday in paradise. She had stood by her principles and resisted short-term pleasures for the long-term gain. Woody's house was hers and her treasures and garden safe.

Lori's thumb worried at her third finger, where the ring had been for so few hours.

She had taken all the advice The Uncles and her cousins and her brother had given her over several years. She had loosened up, lightened up, let her hair down and got herself a man. The only man in an age who'd tempted her away from uninvolvement—and to keep him at arm's length she had married him. After that, not even The Uncles could claim she had no sense of humour.

# CHAPTER SIX

FAIRLIE and Carson's daughter was born in June. Things were looking up, Lori decided at the christening six weeks afterwards. Now there was Fairlie, a strong, wave-making woman, and a new girl-child who would be brought up the same way, Lori didn't feel so lonely in this male bastion. Her loneliness now was of a different kind.

'What do you think of her, Lori?' Carson asked as he beamed down at his tiny daughter cradled in his arms.

It always seemed a daft question to Lori. What *could* one think of six-week-old babies? They were either bald or not bald, crying or not crying, their features as yet unformed, their eyes always blue and any likeness to family members entirely in the minds of onlookers. But she knew her duty.

'She's *beautiful*,' she said of the anonymous bundle that was Felicity Sara Tate. 'And she's taken years off your age. When you married Fairlie you looked ten years younger, and today you look about twenty—in spite of that distinguished silver in your hair. If this goes on, Carson, you'll end up looking as young as your lanky son.'

He grinned and eyed her speculatively. 'I can't say the same for you. You look older since you became a married woman.'

Her heart thumped, but she said calmly enough, 'Gee, thanks, Carson. Why not just come right out and call me a hag?'

'Do you ever see him?'

81

More thumping great heartbeats. She had slipped back into bad habits and was working too hard and drinking too much coffee again. 'Who?' she said coolly, sipping wine from her glass. Was wine any better for irregular heartbeats?

'Your husband.'

*Husband.* Lori blinked rapidly. 'I think of him as a business partner, and no, I haven't seen him since—' She waved a hand, letting the gesture stand for that crazy wedding, warm with the kindness of strangers who had welcomed her into the circle of Haze's family and friends.

They would all know now that it had been a sham, a mere business arrangement. They would probably feel cheated, hoodwinked at having given their affection to a fake. It was months ago but she still had a lingering uneasiness about all those generous people. She cared what they thought about her. Lori wished she could explain to Haze's mother and his sister.

Such asinine meanderings always ended with a sharp reminder that any deception was not her doing. If they had had any false expectations about his marriage, that was Haze's fault for making a wedding of a mere marriage ceremony.

She wondered if his family were as curious about it as her own. The Uncles, initially flabbergasted, never let an opportunity pass without mentioning 'Lorelei's man'. Uncle Clark, horrified that Lori had married without a pre-nuptial agreement, had had Tate's lawyers draw up papers right away. Ritchie, married himself to a well-connected girl of excellent family and prospects, had said he was repelled at the notion of marriage as a means of personal advancement, and Mark had never forgiven her.

'I thought you weren't the marrying kind?' he had accused, as if he should have been able to depend on that. 'You're a cold fish, marrying just to get hold of Woody's place.' And when this had apparently failed to upset her composure, he had attacked from a different angle. 'What kind of a wimp would marry a woman for her money, anyway? Do you have him on a leash, Lorelei?'

She wondered how Mark would react to the 'wimp' in person. No one who had met Haze would ever use his name and the phrase 'on a leash' in the same sentence. Maliciously, she wished Haze would materialise, just to confound The Uncles and her cousins and Mark. Then again, maybe he wouldn't confound them. The Tates were an intimidating bunch who had cut many a big man down to size.

'Where did you get married?' Carson asked now, not for the first time. Carson and Fairlie had a certain look in their eyes when they mentioned her marriage, as if they suspected there might be more to it.

Mark joined them just then. 'Where do you think our Lorelei got married? In some grey little registry office with some grey little man droning out a few unimaginative words. Quick and efficient, that's our Lorelei. I'll bet you even wore one of those suits we see you in at the office, didn't you, pet?'

Lori choked a little on her wine. 'Yes, as a matter of fact I did,' she agreed.

Lori drifted off a little at that, as she sometimes did at recollections of the wedding that should have been very much as Mark described it but in fact had been warmed by affection, perfumed by tuberoses and accompanied by the silver notes of bell-birds.

The weather grew chillier and wetter. Carson announced that he wanted a lesser workload so that he and his family could travel with Fairlie's coming exhibitions. His position as head of Colussus would be up for grabs in a matter of months. Ritchie and Mark geared up to compete for the plum job, but Lori, who had always wanted it, found herself less than ardent about it.

Perhaps it was because, for the first time, she had a proper home here in Melbourne. Woody's place.

It was three months since she'd struck her bargain with Haze. He had never returned the nuptial agreement papers that the Tate lawyers had sent him, and as she had not heard from him she assumed Justine was still tied to her divorce-shy husband. Had they moved in together? She would never know and a good thing too, she told herself as she worked on restoring Woody's bookshelves one freezing, windy night in mid-August. The boughs of the almond tree were slapping against the eaves, and Lori only just heard the thready note of the doorbell over the noise.

A woman stood on the porch. A thin, white-faced woman with dark circles under her eyes and lank hair drooping beneath a purple Annie Hall hat. 'Lori,' she said. It was Haze's sister, Jackie.

'I hope you don't mind but I just don't know anyone in Melbourne and I can't keep taking Amanda into the hospital. It's too distressing, and she's so upset she's started sucking her thumb again and she hasn't done that since she was two, and now she has an earache, so I can't leave her with a stranger and she really liked you, so I—Amanda's in the car. And I'm pregnant,' she wailed. 'That's the good news,' she added with a shadowy version of her smile.

*Hospital?* A superstitious fear seized her. Dazed, she switched on the exterior lights as Jackie darted outside to return a moment later with a tear-stained Amanda, also wearing a felt hat with a daisy. She took her thumb out of her mouth long enough to smile and say, 'Auntie Lori!'

Something turned over inside Lori at this greeting from a distressed child who had only seen her once, three months ago. She kissed the little girl's freckled cheek and said hoarsely, 'What do you mean, hospital?' All those excursions into deserts, mountains, icy wastelands by a man who pushed survival to its limits. 'Has something happened to Haze?'

Jackie clasped her arm in reassurance. 'No, no. He's up in the gulf country—consultant to some film company on location. But of course you'd know that. He's flying down tonight. Oh, you probably know that too. I'm not thinking straight.'

Lori's relief was inordinate. For a moment she had pictured Haze, motionless and pale in a hospital bed, an image that brought back old superstitious fears and new ones. She settled her visitors in the living room and made tea for Jackie, warmed milk for Amanda. 'Flying down tonight...' The gulf country was a continent away. How long did the journey take? Lori's heart pounded. She put some extra milk on to heat for herself. She really must not have any more caffeine.

The cosy interior and the hot drinks had a calming effect on her guests. The words stopped tumbling pell-mell from Jackie's mouth and she leaned back exhausted and told Lori that her husband had had an accident here in Melbourne during a stop-over between flights and was in hospital in Intensive Care. 'They have a place for relatives to stay there and they're very kind, but I just had to get away from the hospital for a little while.' She looked at her daughter who was already brighter, roaming around peering at Woody's books on plants and Lori's collection of miniature antique bottles. 'I hope you don't mind.'

Whether she minded or not seemed hardly relevant. Jackie was hardly recognisable from the laughing, exuberant woman Lori remembered, and anyone with an ounce of humanity would want to help a frightened woman and child. 'I know. A hospital can be a bleak place... I have spare rooms,' she heard herself say. 'You and Amanda must spend the nights with me until Robert gets better.'

Jackie burst into tears. Amanda went to her and they clung together, hats joined. 'Oh, I hoped you'd say that. I couldn't stand a hotel just now...so impersonal...and I'm only two months with the baby and still feeling sick in the mornings, and it's all so...thanks, Lori. You're a darling; I knew you would be.'

'You must be psychic,' Lori said drily. 'You only met me for one day when I hardly said a word apart from "I will".' She bit her lip and flushed, cursing the flippant remark. But it achieved her aim, which had been to lighten the atmosphere.

Jackie laughed and dried her tears and Amanda followed suit. And if Jackie had any questions about the curious state of her brother's marriage, she didn't ask them as Lori bustled about with towels and bedlinen and extra pillows.

Amanda was awake half the night, crying from the pain in her ear, and only got to sleep a couple of hours before dawn. As a queasy Jackie fretted between her need to stay with her sleeping daughter and go to her injured husband, Lori took over. 'Leave Amanda with me. I'll reorganise my appointments and work at home,' she said, bundling Jackie into the hire car she'd arrived in the night before. 'Here's my home number—phone me later if it makes you feel better.'

Maybe when she heard from Jackie she would find out if Haze had arrived at the hospital. Would she get to see him? she wondered. The thought was so disturbing that she had to rearrange the accessories on her study-desk twice before she felt calm enough to get on with some paperwork.

But later it was not Jackie who phoned but Lori's secretary, to say that one of her morning appointments could not be reorganised and that she would have to stand in for Mark later that day at the presentation of a Tate-sponsored sport trophy.

Lori took stock. Amanda was awake, refreshed, bright-eyed and tucking into a huge bowl of cereal. Her ear wasn't aching at all, she told Lori.

'Then how would you like to come to my office with me?'

Amanda liked. But when she entered the imposing Tate building, with its soaring ceilings, stark granite and marble surfaces and giant modern sculptures, Amanda's thumb went into her mouth.

'It affects me a bit like that too sometimes,' Lori said drily, holding the little girl's hand. Cheerfully she introduced her charge to several Tate's personnel, who looked dumbfounded at this new image of the firm's woman director with a plain little ginger-haired girl in tow. There would be plenty of criticism about this, Lori thought. A child in the hallowed halls of the Tate empire, where no child had been before. But that couldn't be helped.

Lori saw her ten-thirty appointment out to the elevator foyer. Relieved, she turned as the doors closed to go and check on Amanda. A vibrant flash of colour in the pale marbled elegance caught her attention. As she hurried on her way the view shifted, and she glimpsed a male back clad in a bright patterned jacket that looked as if it were made from a blanket. A renegade here, where anything but grey suits was rarely seen.

Lori came to an abrupt halt. 'He's flying down...' She glanced back at the exact shape of the man's wide shoulders. But the back of this man's neck was cropped and unfamiliar.

She let out a breath and detoured to her office, poured some coffee as a remedy for a suddenly dry throat. This was so stupid! Haze was probably at this minute by his sister's side at the hospital. She drank some coffee, looked over the rim of the cup. The coloured jacket and its dynamic contents were in her office doorway. Darkest blue eyes fixed on her. Her pulse thundered. She swallowed unwarily and coughed.

His hair had been cut short, so short that the stubble on his face seemed almost as long. He had the jacket open, his hands shoved into jeans pockets. A dark green, almost black T-shirt hugged his chest. If anything it had shrunk since last she'd seen it—the T-shirt, not the chest. No, not the chest, nor the shoulders. He was baggy-eyed, unshaven, scruffy and dressed like an outdated hippie, and he stood there with a hard, arrogant look as if he couldn't give a damn what anyone in this place thought of him.

He looked great—but then, a man who could rate nine out of ten in a wetsuit would. The man also looked accusing, she realised, though just what he was accusing her of, she couldn't imagine. He'd got the funds to pay his tax, and his business was safe, wasn't it? He'd been free to carry on his liaison with Justine, hadn't he? She'd kept her part of the bargain, so what the hell was he looking like that for?

Lori put the coffee-cup on her desk with a thump. 'Hasn't that thing worn out yet?' she said, indicating the T-shirt.

He looked down. 'What thing do you mean?'

She flushed. Crude devil.

'Surely the financial deal I arranged can accommodate a new T-shirt.' She winced inwardly, but it was too late to recall the words.

Haze's mouth tilted sardonically. 'Are you fishing for gratitude, Lori?' he said. 'You won't get it. You've done me no favours, just repaid me for helping you win yourself a fortune.'

'I didn't mean—' she began, but he came into the office, looking around at the framed certificates, awards and photographs that plotted her career since she was twenty.

'Impressive,' he said, stopping at last at a group photo. 'Is this a boyfriend? I thought you didn't have time for boyfriends. Although I suppose a man comes in handy when you get an invitation that says "and partner".'

It was a photograph taken many years ago, of her with a Tate's executive—long departed to a rival group of companies. The Uncles and the current Prime Minister were also in the frame.

'His name is Carl,' she said, furtively studying the back of his neck. All that thick, long hair was gone. She felt a small pang of protest.

He lifted the picture off the wall and regarded it critically. If she remembered rightly, the man Carl had photographed particularly well—his figure elegant in a dove-grey three-piece suit, his hair receding but soft and refined, unlike either Haze's former shoulder-length hair or his current vigorous nap. Carl had been a colleague, not a boyfriend, but he'd had his hand at her waist in the photograph. No need for Haze to know that it had meant nothing.

'One of the survivors, hmm?'

'What?' she asked, dragging her eyes from the forceful breadth of his back as he turned. 'Oh, I see what you mean.' She winced. 'Yes, I didn't put a hex on Carl.' Quite true. She could hardly remember a thing about the man except that he'd had a wife and at least two children.

'Snappy dresser,' he said. 'Looks the academic type.'

'Carl was—is—a very cultured man,' she said carefully.

'The right kind of guy for your kind of life—a bit stuffy, maybe, a bit on the dull side? Why didn't you marry him?'

She plucked the photograph from his hand, restored it to its place on the wall. 'He was already married,' she said.

His expression was surprised, even distasteful. 'Oh, I see. You can have an affair with a married woman, but if I have one with a married man that makes me some kind of homewrecker?'

Except that she hadn't had an affair with a married man and never would. Lori bit her lip. This mix of truth and fiction was idiotic, and she wished she'd never started it. But she rather liked having her own antidote to Justine. 'I can't imagine why you would think he's stuffy and dull. Or that my life might be, for that matter.'

'Look at the clues,' he invited, with an expansive sweep of one arm. 'Show me a stuffier, duller office if you can. Look at yourself.' He looked with great thoroughness, taking in her pin-striped suit, her cream shirt, her drawn-back hair.

Lori gritted her teeth. 'I am over-supplied with males who feel entitled to criticise what I wear, thanks. You're the self-styled survival expert—hasn't it occurred to you that I dress this way in order to blend in with a hostile environment?'

'And do you blend in?' he asked, as if he knew that she did not and that it mattered to her. Lori felt a strong desire to hit him. 'Anyway,' he went on, 'stuffy and dull it may be, but this is an exclusive little world you live in, hardly a survival situation. If it were, any expert—even a *self-styled* expert—would tell you that only a fool or a coward tries to blend in to a hostile environment. To survive you have to take care, but you also have to take risks.'

Lori felt the blood rush to her face. It was one thing to wonder if she'd been a fool to waste years of her working life trying to find a place for herself here, trying to make a difference in this male jungle. But a coward? She'd never lacked courage. Being scared had never stopped her from trying.

Hands on hips, Lori met his eyes levelly. 'I take it you had some point to make about—um—' she gestured at the photograph of the supposed lover whose name was escaping her '—Carl, before you flee my stuffy, dull office?'

The man had the nerve to grin. For once she felt able to resist the attraction of it.

'I can't help noticing that I am the direct opposite of him.'

It was said with the casual arrogance of a man accustomed to physical superiority. Carl was shorter, slighter, losing his hair. In the charisma stakes Haze was way ahead. She didn't remember even liking Carl very much, but now she felt angry on his behalf. 'Oh, I dare say you'd beat him in hand-wrestling,' she said scathingly. 'But Carl doesn't go in for macho boys' games. He's the cerebral type—as you pointed out.'

It was true about Carl, but the insinuation that Haze was all muscle between the ears was not. All the same, she saw with malicious pleasure that it had stung him. There was a delicate wash of colour high on his cheeks. He looked moodily over at the photograph, and his speech slowed down as if he was thinking out loud. 'I've often wondered why you seemed at first as if you—' He turned and looked at her. 'You saw me as a bit down-market, I suppose—a long-haired gypsy but exciting—'

She rolled her eyes. 'Is there a man alive who *doesn't* think he's exciting?'

'Not what you were used to—unpredictable,' he went on, as if she hadn't spoken.

Lori snorted. 'Well, it's true I've never met a man before who hacked open a coconut as a prelude to a dinner invitation!'

'You were titillated from the moment we met,' he continued, biting out the words with more certainty as he went on. 'Staring at my long hair—I don't suppose the men you know ever let their hair grow—and you were fascinated with my tattoo...'

Lori flushed, thinking it was less the tattoo that had fascinated than the man it marked. 'Your imagination is as vivid as your jacket!' she said.

Haze came up close to her, studying her with insulting detachment, as if she were a specimen of some form of life he was coming to grips with. 'A man with calluses on his hands—' He turned his palms out, and part of her admired the strong, graceful lines of his hands and wrists. He placed those hands either side of her, on the wall, hemming her in. 'You were tempted there for a while, weren't you? I was something of a novelty for the rich Ms Tate, used to city men.' His voice dropped very low. 'Almost, you might say, rough trade.'

Lori gasped. Her growing urge to hit him reached a peak and she swiped at him. His hand came up in a blur and blockaded the blow, pushing aside her arm as he moved in close, preventing any further attempts to hit him by pinning her against the wall with his bulk. Darkest blue eyes glared into hers. His nostrils dilated with the deep, gusting breaths he took.

'But in the end you got cold feet and calmly went back to your luxury holiday hideaway and thought up another, creative way to use me. Because, one way or another, I was going to be of use to you, wasn't I? You're a Tate, and the Tates don't waste time on anything or anyone that doesn't show a profit.'

'No,' she said huskily, conscious of his heat and the muscular contours of his torso and thighs pressing against her. She was hot and claustrophobic, her only horizon a dazzling wrap-around of rough wool, patterned with Navajo markings of terracotta, yellow and turquoise. 'You make me sound mercenary, and I wasn't—'

'No?' he growled. 'What were those papers your lawyers sent me, then? That *nuptial agreement*.' He said it as if only pond slime were more contemptible. 'Were you worried that I might suddenly divorce you and sue for alimony? Get myself a bit of the famous Tate money?'

'That wasn't me—I said it wasn't necessary, but Uncle Clark— I didn't know he'd sent it on.'

His body inched forward, flattening her against the wall.

'Well, maybe I have a few clauses to add to it myself, my devoted wife,' he sneered. 'After all, I have to protect *my* assets too. You career-types want it all—you might suddenly hear the ticking of your biological clock and decide you want a baby, all included in the price. Stud performances, honey, are extra.'

She let out a strangled cry of rage and kicked him. The toe of her shoe connected with his shin.

'Ow—bloody hell!' he said, screwing up his eyes.

'I hope it hurts, you arrogant pig. You're quite safe. If my biological clock should start ticking, I wouldn't call on *your*—' She perceived that she had talked herself into a corner in her temper.

He opened one eye and said, 'Services?' in such a tone that Lori was visited by a graphic vision of the nature of his services. Her face flushed deeply. 'Assets?' he murmured. More graphic visions, of a kind she'd never had anywhere—least of all in the office where she was conscious of the critical scrutiny of the male Tates. She had a superstitious fear that if she didn't get him out of her office soon her private visions might become public by some process of osmosis.

'I have work to do,' she said, resolutely breaking eye contact. Relax. She used the word to regulate her breathing. *Re*—breathe in—*lax*—breathe out. It usually worked.

Haze didn't move, kept her fenced up against the wall with a superabundance of muscle and thick, coarse wool. He watched her efforts at self-discipline with keen interest.

'Look at that,' he said mockingly. 'From real live woman to a cold business machine, right before my very eyes.'

She'd heard many versions of the insult, but it stung her anew. 'You men are never satisfied, are you?' she hissed. 'If I wear pretty clothes I'm unprofessional—maybe even provocative. If I don't I'm aggressive and unfeminine. If I lose my cool in the office I'm emotional and unreliable. If I don't I'm a cold business machine. I wish you would all grow up!'

His solidity, his strength that so casually held her captive within a tiny space, suddenly filled her with frustration, even loathing. Fiercely she pushed at him, horrified when tears welled in her eyes.

Haze blinked, looked at her trembling mouth.

'Laura-love,' he said softly, brushing the backs of his fingers over her cheek.

'Don't call me *Laura*,' she said childishly, turning away from that tantalising touch. Don't call me *love*, she added silently.

He touched her hair briefly, brushed his thumb over her lower lip. Then he bent his head and lightly pressed his mouth to hers in the kind of kiss one might give a child for comfort. He withdrew and stared down at her.

She was shaken by that chaste kiss; she couldn't think why. Her hands clutched at the thick lapels of his jacket. Tremors went through her body. When he hauled her from the wall into his arms she was already melting in to him, her hands sliding up over his shoulders, her lips seeking his. And this was no child-like kiss but an earth-shaking statement of raw desire, a possession symbolic of another, yet untasted. She groaned, winding herself close around him, feeling the ache for him deep down in her, a sweet, tormenting pain.

'Ms Tate—oh!' The voice stopped abruptly. Haze slowly lifted his head. Lori saw that it was one of her staff who stood there, her face red even as she avidly took in every detail of the tableau. 'The door was open, so I'm afraid—'

'That's OK,' Haze said easily, without releasing Lori. He had a foot planted between hers and his hands on her upper thighs, crushing folds of her skirt. 'I'm just saying hello to my wife. Haven't seen her for a while.'

The woman went out, big with news. At last, a glimpse of the rumoured husband of the director. Within hours everyone at Tate's would be talking about Lorelei Tate's husband—the big, handsome, oversexed brute with a lousy taste in clothes.

Released at last, Lori groaned. All these years she had kept her minimal private life strictly out of sight, and now she had to be apprehended in a clinch with a big, unshaven oaf with her skirt hitched up and her hair in disarray.

'Did you have to say that?' she said sharply. 'Now it will be all over the office.'

He smirked. 'You'd rather it be all around the office that you were almost ravishing a man who *isn't* your husband?'

'It wasn't *me* doing the ravishing,' she hissed. 'You big brute—you had me up against the wall.'

'You underestimate yourself. If we'd had no interruptions, by now I dare say you'd have me on your couch over there. I really must draft that phrase to add to our nuptial agreement,' he said provokingly.

Lori resisted the provocation, straightened her clothes, consulted the mirror inside her clothes cabinet briefly to tidy her hair. Haze wandered about, picked up a hard hat and looked questioningly at her.

'Sometimes I have to visit building sites,' she said.

Haze tapped the reinforced surface of the helmet. 'And this is harder than your head?' he mocked.

Lori closed the cabinet door with a hard-won restraint. 'I'm busy, Haze.'

He tossed the helmet down. 'This wasn't intended as a—social call,' he said. 'I'm here about Amanda.'

Lori looked blankly at him, stricken that she had temporarily forgotten that of course that was why he was here. As she hastily disguised her expression he said sardonically, 'You do remember Amanda—my niece? Small, ginger-haired girl you volunteered to nurture today?'

Lori shot him a look of pure dislike. For a while there *he* hadn't seemed to remember his niece either, but that didn't seem to bother him. As usual, one rule for a man—another for a woman.

'Jackie is under the impression that her daughter is safely at your home in your tender, loving care,' he said with a cynical smile. 'I phoned, and when I got no answer guessed you'd abandoned that homely option—if you ever meant to take it. So where has the busy lady director dumped my niece while she attends to business?'

Lori felt a spasm of guilt in spite of herself, but threw him a frosty look and marched from her office. He followed her.

'You might have had the decency to take her back to her mother at the hospital rather than leave her with strangers. I don't think you understand what she and Jackie are going through,' he said, catching her arm and bringing her to a halt in view of several fascinated staff. Lori saw the word 'husband' framed on their lips, and earthy feminine interest in their eyes. 'If you've caused her any unnecessary pain, I'll—' He bit off the words and Lori's anger diminished a fraction as she realised that he was more anxious than he appeared.

'Is Robert any better this morning?' she asked.

'No worse, so that's something.'

'I do know what it's like,' she said shortly. 'I was older than Amanda when my mother went to hospital, and I remember only too well just how...' She crushed a horde of memories, and went on briskly. 'Just how frightening it was.'

She led the way to step over a red and gold cordon to open one of two large timber doors carved with the Tate logo.

'Here's where I *dumped* your niece,' she said tensely. She was going to feel rotten if little Amanda was crying her eyes out with distress or earache or both—and not only because her Uncle Haze would regard her, Lori, as some piece of low-life.

She need not have worried. Amanda was happily engaged in something that had her crouched over the table with Mary Crombie, the administrative supervisor. On the floor, twin tracks in the sumptuous silk carpet led a long and circuitous way to the other end of the room, where an orange toy truck was parked.

Haze looked at the massive table, cluttered with paper and colored pens, a carton of milk with a straw stuck in it, a plate holding biscuit crumbs. Amanda's doll, Becky, was perched at the head of the table—in Uncle Clark's place, Lori saw. She smiled, thinking of her unsuccessful attempt to get another woman on the board. Maybe it was an omen.

'The boardroom?' Haze said, his mouth twitching. He turned a speculative look on Lori. 'Bringing a baby to work with you—is that a good career move, Ms Tate?'

And even now, when he could see that she was doing her best for Amanda, the man was being sarcastic and critical. 'I'll survive,' she said briskly. 'Now that you're here, you can take her off my hands. I'm really too busy to be babysitting.'

But her cool pose was entirely ruined when Amanda saw them and came running into her uncle's arms. 'Uncle Haze—Auntie Lori let me see her office where she works, and she has *three* phones, and she let me talk on them and press all the buttons.'

'Did she, possum?' Haze murmured, looking at Lori over his niece's head.

'And she said that her and I—that Auntie Lori and me—are the only girls to ever sit at this table and be bored—only I wasn't bored. I made something for Auntie Lori with Mary...' She wriggled down and ran to confer with Mary over something on the table.

Haze grinned suddenly, and Lori nearly jumped out of her skin. She'd forgotten, she really had, just how much energy that flashing smile of his created. 'Your wayward sense of humor, Lori? What would The Uncles think?'

'That it was sacrilege,' she said drily. 'Almost as bad as having a pregnant woman in the boardroom.'

His eyebrows shot up. 'Pregnant?' he said.

He seemed discomfited, and Lori thought it served him right. All those insulting remarks about her using him as a stud male.

'One of the many reservations The Uncles had about a female candidate for the board recently. The woman might decide to have a baby, and they felt it would be inadvisable to risk such a shocking thing as a pregnant woman in the boardroom. They chose a man instead.'

'Ah.'

Tension hung over them. Lori's mind wandered. What would a child of his be like? she wondered. Tough. Resilient. Affectionate, she thought, thinking of Haze with his family. Would Justine want to have another child with Haze as the father? It jolted her. Lori found it all too easy to lose sight of Justine.

Amanda finally completed her conference with Mary and came running, something glittering in her hands.

'This is for you, Auntie Lori,' she said. 'It's a necklace.'

It was made of intertwined paperclips, each one bound with a tiny strip of flowered contact plastic and clipped into a chain, with a makeshift tassel of several lengths of more shiny clips. 'Mary helped me. Put it on.'

Lori knelt down and the necklace was laid over her head. Its bright turquoise and purple plastic lay garishly on her burgundy pin-striped suit. 'Thank you, Amanda. You've made it beautifully,' she said. 'Now, get your doll. I think your uncle would like to take you to see Mummy and Daddy.'

Amanda put her thumb in her mouth. She fetched her doll and kissed Mary Crombie goodbye, and came back to Haze very subdued. Even when he picked her up and held her close in strong arms surely guaranteed to make anyone feel secure, Lori thought, the little girl was worried. 'Will my Daddy die?' she said at last, and Lori felt as if someone had punched her in the chest.

Haze hugged her and said comforting, positive things, but Amanda kept demanding the one promise he couldn't bring himself to make—that her father would not die. As they left Amanda twisted around to see Lori. 'Will you wear my necklace today, Auntie Lori?' she said, with a wobbling lower lip. 'Will you wear it *all* the whole day? Do you promise?'

Lori hesitated, but took the child's hand and said solemnly, 'I promise to wear your necklace all the whole day, Amanda.'

'And not take it off at all?'

'Not until I have a shower tonight.'

Amanda smiled, as if her world was a little more secure now that a grown-up had made a promise about something. Haze nodded goodbye, and he looked both grateful that she had treated the little girl's plea seriously and sceptical. He made a swift comparison of her excellent tailoring with the gaudy, glittering necklace, and his expression said that he knew the paperclip jewellery wouldn't last five minutes after Amanda was gone.

Lori went back to her office, furtively watching Haze on his way to the lobby as he appeared and reappeared between marble pillars, carrying his niece.

Did men know, she wondered, just how appealing they looked with a child in their arms? Maybe it was the contrast between male strength and childish weakness, the sight of a small hand laid trustingly on a muscular arm. Maybe it was seeing all that strength, with its potential for dominance and violence, being used in tender support that was so moving. He was gone from her sight at last and she sighed, released from fascination.

This was one place she'd never expected to see him. She hesitated at her door as she heard the hushed sound of elevator doors, and idiotically she had to wait for them to close again before she turned into her office. It was the plight of the little girl that had her hands trembling, she decided. It was traumatic, bringing back pain she had long thought resolved. But it wasn't just that. There was a descant to this turmoil, a soaring excitement along with the rest.

After months of going through the motions in her organised life, she felt confused, angry, disappointed, sad, yet oddly wanting to laugh. Anticipation of heaven knew what pounded in her veins. She hated this awful lack of control, not knowing what would happen next, but she felt fully awake, alive, coursing with energy.

# CHAPTER SEVEN

THAT day, for the first time in years, Lori went home early. She made the Tate trophy presentation at a youth sports carnival, complete with brass band and media coverage, and instead of returning to the office, as she would have usually, she went home, wondering if Haze, Jackie and Amanda would be there. Jackie, after all, had a key.

Lori wasn't sure how she felt about Haze prowling around in her house, making himself familiar with her private domain. And she could hardly order him out, could she, when his sister and niece were live-in guests? Whatever had happened to her architecturally symmetrical plan? It had begun to come apart the moment she was embraced by the Callahan family.

But the house was empty. She did some chores, plumped cushions and obsessively tidied Woody's treasures and her own. People did things like that to give themselves a feeling of control, experts said. Arranging inanimate things was a substitute for being able to arrange more difficult things satisfactorily. Like certain people. Like feelings for certain people that were quite clearly absurd. She detected one of her Victorian green bottles out of alignment and went back to fix it before she went to the bathroom.

A shower restored her somewhat. She emerged in a cloud of steam, her frangipani-printed robe wrapped around her. When a hulking shape loomed up before her in the unlit passageway she let out a screech and backed up on the slippery bathroom floor, clutching at the towel-rail for support.

'It's only me,' Haze said sardonically. 'One of the good guys. Here—' He hauled her upright and stood close, looking down at her, breathing in the steamy, scented air, holding it for a moment. He had an army-style tote bag on his back, the webbing strap diagonally slicing across the garish wool jacket.

Lori clapped a hand to her thundering heart. 'Of all the *stupid* things to do,' she snapped, hearing the abnormally high pitch of her voice. 'Looming up in the mist like—like Jack the Ripper.'

'I'm unarmed,' he said drily. After a few thoughtful moments, he bent and picked her up. A faint grunt escaped him.

'There's no need for that,' she said as her feet left the floor. 'I was startled, that's all. Couldn't you have knocked?'

'I was about to knock when you opened the door. Which way is the bedroom?'

Her heart lurched. 'I'm not immobilised. Put me down!'

'Is it an affront to your independence to be carried? Am I being politically incorrect, picking you up?'

There was nothing political about her objections. She desperately wanted him to put her down before he felt the violent thud of her heart. The thin robe was all she wore, and she might as well have been naked in his arms. Lori needed at least a fully lined business suit between herself and Haze Callahan. The mist was clearing and there they were, reflected in the mirror.

He staggered slightly and she said, 'Look, put me down before you drop me. When the hero sweeps a woman into his arms he's supposed to make it look effortless, not turn red in the face and totter.'

He shifted, tossing her slightly to improve his balance. 'I am carrying a tote bag as well,' he said, aggrieved. 'And you aren't exactly thistledown.'

As he tramped from the bathroom her foot scraped the vanity basin and something rattled as it slid across the counter and hit the tiled splashback. Haze glanced down, thrusting out his lips at the coiled splendour of the paperclip necklace made by Amanda.

'You've got an eye for detail,' he said with a sardonic smile. 'When Amanda sees that here, she'll assume you really *did* wear it until you took your shower.'

Her mouth compressed. 'The cords on your neck are standing out,' she observed. 'You'd better put me down.'

Haze smiled, flexed his muscles and tossed her yet again, to achieve a more comfortable hold. 'Which way?' he said.

She ground her teeth. 'This is one of those prehistoric male techniques for dominance in new territory, is it? Flexing your superior muscles?'

He stopped smiling. 'Your bedroom—to the right or left?' he said, and she recognised the immovability of a man determined to get his own way.

'Oh, for heaven's sake! That way!' she snapped, pointing to the right.

Amanda came in just then, and close behind her was Jackie, who grabbed her by the hand when she saw Lori in her brother's arms. 'Come on, Amanda,' she said, exchanging a wink with Haze. 'Let's give this pair some privacy. Uncle Haze has been away for a week.'

He found her bedroom and walked in, pushed the door shut behind with one foot, then dropped Lori on the quilted queen-sized bed. With a groaning sigh he raised the strap and shed the tote bag, which landed with a thump on the floor. Lori stared up at him as he glanced around the room with its swagged muslin curtains and fine old Persian rug. He went over to her bureau, leaned across it to study the framed photographs of her marathon finishes in London, Boston, Tokyo. There was a gratifying respect in his eyes.

'A week?' Lori said. 'What does she mean?'

He shrugged, picked up an ornate double picture frame with two photographs. 'Your parents?'

She nodded. Haze flicked his gaze back and forth, comparing her with the pictures.

'You look like your mother. How old were you when she—?'

'Nine,' she broke in. 'She had a virus that attacked the heart muscle and had a transplant. She lived for a year afterwards but was never really well again...always in hospital.'

Haze pulled his mouth down. 'You really do understand how it is for Jackie and Amanda. I apologise for suggesting you couldn't.'

For some reason she felt angry rather than mollified by his apology. 'Yes, I do understand how it is—visiting the hospital day after day until...'

Haze looked hard at her, waiting without words in that way he had, and though she never talked about it, she found herself going on. 'I didn't know, you see, that she'd died. Had convinced myself it wasn't possible because Dad had promised me nothing would happen to her. My father didn't get the message and we went to visit. I ran on ahead and found my mother's bed empty. I just thought they'd moved her to another room, so I started looking for her.'

'And you were nine. That's tough. Where was your brother?'

'At boarding-school,' she said absently, eyes on the photographs. 'Poor Dad. He was told his wife had died and then his daughter went missing for hours.'

'Hours?' Haze said.

'It takes a long time to search a hospital,' she said, taking the picture from his hand. 'I don't like hospitals much.'

Meticulously she repositioned it on her dressing table, shifting her hairbrush until it was exactly parallel with the frame. She felt Haze watching, and turned.

'I like things to be neat,' she said defensively.

'Yeah,' he said with a grin. 'And at your age you can't go about sucking your thumb.'

As she fumed at this nonchalant piece of amateur psychology, so near to the truth, he sat on the edge of the bed and unlaced his boots. The implied intimacy of it sent a frisson down her spine.

'You can't take off your boots here—this is my bedroom. Get out—go on.' She pushed at him, but might as well have tried to dislodge Ayers Rock.

'Lori—I'm dead tired,' he said. She supposed there *was* a hint of tiredness in the dynamic stretch of his shoulders as he stripped off the heavy wool jacket. 'Just need a nap. Travelling most of the night and got no sleep.'

'Well, you can't sleep here,' she said firmly. 'I'll phone a hotel and book you a room.'

Haze toppled sideways like a felled oak. 'Can't go to a hotel,' he said on a long sigh. 'Jackie would think that we—um. Too tired to go to a hotel tonight.'

'Jackie would think that we—what?' she demanded. Suddenly several things slotted into place. 'Of course you'd know that', Jackie had said when talking about Haze's schedule. As if she was in constant touch with him. 'Uncle Haze has been away for a week,' Jackie had said when she saw him carrying Lori—a neat little piece of stage-management on his part.

'You—you've let your family think that ours is a real marriage!' Without opening his eyes, he made a lazy gesture with one hand that clearly meant, Later. 'Oh, no—don't think you're going to fob me off, Haze.' She knelt on the bed and shook his arm until he rolled over. 'Does Jackie think you live here with me?'

'Not all the time.' He sighed and opened one eye. 'Only weekends, and odd times when our schedules don't clash.' He dragged both eyelids open and studied her. 'Don't worry about it.'

'Don't *worry* about it?' she snapped. 'I already feel dreadful, pulling the wool over their eyes with that— that ridiculous romantic wedding. I'm not going to be party to deceiving them any further. What on earth can you be thinking?'

He smiled sleepily and reached up to touch her hair, curving his large hand so that it lightly brushed along the side of her face. There was a slow-burning heat in his eyes. 'Right now? Guess,' he said.

It was a good thing she was kneeling on the bed, because her knees felt quite weak. And it was a good thing she had years of practice at refusing to be distracted by the red herrings men liked to draw across the main track. 'Why did you do it?' she insisted, in a voice turned husky.

After a count of six, he said, 'Wishful thinking?'

'Don't be flippant, Haze!' She bent over him as he showed every sign of going to sleep on her bed. 'I demand that you get off my bed and tell your sister right now that we aren't married at all. Well, that we *are* married but that it isn't real—Haze. *Haze!*'

He opened his eyes again at her insistent shaking. His hands came up and caught her around the ribs, neatly looping back the edges of her robe. 'Mmm,' he said, studying her exposed breasts so close above him. 'You smell delicious.' Quickly he raised his head and licked at the tip of one breast, then the other. His mouth fastened and sucked strongly, and his tongue made a lavish, circular farewell. Pure pleasure chased shock through her nervous system. '*Taste* delicious.'

Lori scrambled free, yanked her robe into place. To restore her dignity, she picked up her suit jacket and brushed it, ready to hang in the wardrobe with all the other dignified and orderly ranked jackets. But when she opened the wardrobe door and raked the hangers along, some iridescent green flounces sprang out, stiffened hems a-quiver, so that you could almost hear the sounds of music and girlish laughter. Lori subdued the irrepressible green dress and closed the door.

Propped up with one arm behind his head, Haze laughed, but as she reached the door he said seriously, 'Lori? Don't say anything to Jackie yet. Please? I'll sort it out, OK?'

She went out and closed the door and stood a moment, her hands pressed to her breasts where she tingled from the sly touch of his tongue. Her nipples were tight and indecently obvious beneath her robe. The man had all the gall under the sun, taking advantage like that. No refinement, no reticence. But great deftness and experience and confidence. She curled her lip in contempt, yet felt a sneaking admiration too.

Lori shook her head and hurried into the bathroom, where she indulged in the therapy of straightening towels, re-aligning the soap and loofah. 'Wishful thinking...' Was that remotely possible? That he *wanted* the marriage to be real? But why would he, when there was Justine?

Lori adjusted the row of African violets on the wide window sill. The man had just passed out on her bed and left his clothes lying about on the floor. Untidy, unshaven, unshowered and uninvited. But she knew what really bothered her was that he could be so casually erotic and ruffle her like this. What would it be like if he really *tried*?

When everything in the bathroom was geometrically arranged, she went out to the living room before Jackie started thinking there was a passionate reunion going on in the main bedroom.

She suppressed her irritation at Jackie's arch expression, and asked after Robert. He had improved dramatically this afternoon, Jackie said, which explained her lighter mood. If he remained stable for twelve hours he would be moved from Intensive Care. As she went on to give Lori the details culled from the medical staff Lori's mind wandered to her bedroom, where her

husband was cat-napping on her bed. Just where did he
imagine he was going to sleep tonight?

It was a topic she took up with Haze when he reappeared an hour later, bleary-eyed, in her kitchen, where
she and Jackie were drinking coffee. 'Any coffee going,
Laura-love?' he said, widening his eyes slightly to remind
her that Jackie thought they were a couple.

Lori gave her sweetest smile. 'Help yourself. You know
where everything's kept. Darling.'

Of course he didn't, and Lori enjoyed the few brief
moments while Haze endeavoured to look as if this was
a second home to him. Jackie didn't notice. She took
her coffee and announced that she was going to monitor
what junk her daughter was watching on television.
'We'll turn in soon,' she said with a meaningful look.
'Amanda and I want to be up early to go to the hospital.'

'Cups to your right. Coffee to your left,' Lori said
when his sister had gone. 'I don't intend to keep this
pretence up, so you had better tell your family.'

'Not a good time, don't you think?' he said drily. 'Let's
see Robert out of Intensive Care first.'

He boiled the kettle and made coffee, brought it to
the table and sat opposite her. His gaze wandered around
the kitchen, with its old-fashioned cupboards and walk-
in pantry. Lori had installed a super new oven and work
surfaces, but apart from those improvements the old
kitchen was still basically as Woody had used it.

His gaze came back to fix on her. 'Either this old heap
is built over a goldmine, or I'm wrong about you.'

'You were expecting prize real estate in the broker belt?
Sandstone, marble, thirty rooms and servants' quarters?'

His smile was a touch sheepish. 'Something like that.
I assumed any godparent of yours would have had the
golden touch.'

'The Tates always had the golden touch. Woody was a good friend of my mother. Her family and friends weren't poor, but neither were they rich.'

She saw him glance around again, at the pleasant but homely kitchen.

'Why would an ambitious, independent woman like you abandon her principles and marry to get hold of a place like this?'

'Maybe there *is* a goldmine under the floorboards.'

Haze studied her. 'Why?' he asked softly.

'Maybe it's a *novelty*,' she drawled. 'Maybe I got sick of upmarket apartments with marble foyers and harbour views. Maybe I had a yen for something *rough*.'

His eyes flickered but he didn't respond. 'Why?'

Lori had to admire his singlemindedness of purpose. 'Because,' she said, 'it was the nearest thing to home that I remember when I was growing up. After my mother died, Woody was my confidante, my mentor, my—' she swallowed hard '—my other mother.

'She encouraged me when I doubted I could do what my brother did...and in a family like mine it was easy for a girl to wonder if she had what it took to succeed out there—' Lori waved a hand in the direction of the tough, competitive world beyond Woody's garden. 'Woody always told me I could do whatever I set my heart on. If it hadn't been for her I'm not sure that I could have become what I am now. That's why...'

'That's why?' he prompted.

He genuinely wanted to know. Lori was surprised to find that she genuinely wanted to tell him. 'That's why I can't understand why she made the condition that I marry in her will. She never married herself. She was a landscape gardener, an independent woman running her own business.'

'You could have contested a condition like that, surely?' Haze said.

Lori recoiled. 'Oh, no. It was Woody's wish, and it wouldn't be fair to question the wishes of someone who is—can't argue their case. It would be a betrayal... But I would like to understand *why* she did it.'

He studied her for a long time. 'She left you no explanation?'

Lori shook her head. 'I went through all the drawers, her papers—nothing.'

'Maybe she thought marriage would improve you. Maybe she thought you were getting sour,' he said, amusement pulling at his mouth.

'You make me sound like a pint of milk on the turn!' She glared at him. 'Anyway, now that you've realised this is a small house and not a mansion, you won't be surprised to know that I have no spare bedroom you can use tonight. Being a survival expert, I don't imagine that will present any problem to you.'

'I brought my sleeping bag with me and I can sleep anywhere,' he agreed. 'On the floor in your bedroom, I thought.'

'No,' she said vehemently. She wouldn't get a wink of sleep with him in the same room. And it was such a short distance from the floor to the bed. Or from the bed to the floor, for that matter. She flushed, horrified with this frankly carnal turn of mind. 'You can have the living room couch.'

'And have Jackie thinking our marriage is in jeopardy? Before you knew it my mother would be down here, sorting us out. Believe me, you wouldn't enjoy that.'

'This is ridiculous! The deal is complete and we'll be divorced any time now, anyway!'

He looked scandalised. 'I can't spring a divorce on them while they still think we're made for each other. Be reasonable.'

Lori closed her eyes in resignation. 'I wish you'd take this seriously.' She opened her eyes. 'And how could they think we're made for each other?'

'My mother swears she took one look at us together and knew it,' he said drily. 'When she saw the wedding photos, she was convinced we had a match made in heaven.'

'You mean the photos taken by your friend who specialises in snapping rock-climbers and intrepid bush-walkers?' Lori gave a snort. 'Your mother must be very determined to believe in your fairy-tale marriage. You shouldn't have let it go on.'

'When Robert is out of danger, I'll tell her,' he repeated kindly, as if to a slow child. 'Of course, I can't stop you telling Jackie now. She'll probably move out when you do. Back to the soulless hospital accommodation with her morning sickness and poor little Amanda with an earache.'

Lori stoically resisted the blatant play for compassion.

'Not necessarily. I'm sure she thinks of me as a friend.'

'She thinks of you as family. She won't feel she can take your hospitality when she finds out you are simply her brother's business partner. It would go against family loyalty, if you can imagine such a thing.'

Lori glared at him. 'You are manipulating me.'

'That's right,' he said cheerfully. 'Playing on your finer feelings.'

'I wasn't aware you thought I _had_ any finer feelings,' she retorted.

'You aren't aware of a lot of things, Laura-love.'

Wherever he slept that night, it wasn't in her room. And, much to her annoyance, his absence proved just as distracting as his presence. He wasn't in the house—a fact she established as she ghosted around at one in the morning, looking in the laundry and larger cupboards. As if she was likely to come across a big blue-eyed man in pyjamas nestled in with the raincoats, umbrellas and gumboots. He probably didn't wear pyjamas anyway.

It was not a train of thought to bring serenity. She tossed on her bed and got up several times to peer from her window. The winds that night had come directly across Antarctic ice floes, and she felt a twinge of guilt. The poor man had already had one terrible night.

But in the morning, when she ventured into the kitchen, it was she who was wan and baggy-eyed. Haze was seated at her kitchen table, the newspaper, a pen and some handwritten notes in front of him. A book of poetry was trapped in sunlight, an envelope marking a place one quarter of the way through. The paper-free surfaces were cluttered with plates bearing traces of egg and toast crumbs.

He looked hale and hearty, the whites of his eyes dazzling, the blue intense. Black hair. Golden tanned skin. Lori wondered if she was still asleep. But didn't the experts say you never dreamed in colour? Shoulders, broad. Jaw, newly shaven. His beautiful, strong right hand curved around a coffee-mug. The other was hooked over a chair-back in a bright spear of sunlight lancing through the casement window. Lori stared at the persuasive contours of his forearm, at the hundreds of tiny hairs burnished by the sun.

Pulled to one side, the open collar of his drill shirt framed a columned neck and a glimpse of collarbone. He was so solid, so good to look at, so vividly *alive*. The old superstitious anxiety made her fidget. Could it possibly be true that some people, fortunate themselves, carried bad luck to others—a sort of Typhoid Mary? He moved, and the sunlight flashed on his heavy wristwatch.

She blinked, pulled herself together.

'I borrowed a book—I hope you don't mind.' He pointed to the book on the table, one of Woody's.

She made a non-committal sound and fingered the worn binding of the book.

'There's an old gas bill stuck in the pages,' he said, indicating the bookmark.

With deliberation, she pushed the book and his notes aside, clearing her usual place at the table. It bothered her, this casual occupation of her space. His boots on the floor beside her bed, his jacket sprawled across her chair, his notes scattered on her kitchen table. Lori frowned, feeling especially bad-tempered this morning. She took a pencil from a shelf, laid it parallel with a spoon on the table.

'I hope you haven't done my crossword,' she said.

The newspaper rustled as he ostentatiously folded it at the crossword page and set it next to her pencil. 'Not a morning person, then, Laura-love?' A brilliant smile intensified the impression of rampant good health.

'Why are cheerful risers always so darned patronising to the rest of us?' Peevishly she poured some muesli into a bowl, added milk. 'Where did you sleep last night, anyway?' she said accusingly, as if the site might be responsible for this unnatural morning heartiness.

'In your garden shed.'

'In the shed?' she exclaimed, looking out of the window. 'But there's a bag of manure in there... and lawn fertiliser. And it's draughty.'

'It was a bit on the fragrant side,' he admitted. 'But cosy compared with some places I've had to sleep.'

And he'd obviously showered since, for he had brought no elusive smells of ripening chicken manure into the kitchen. She worked her jaws resolutely over the toasted muesli and allotted herself the usual five minutes with the crossword. Haze returned to his notes and there was silence save for the tiny sounds of his pen moving over paper, and Lori discovered an unexpected serenity in sharing a table with him in her sunny kitchen. He put down his pen as she abandoned the crossword.

'Jackie and Amanda—' she said, suddenly realising that the house was too quiet.

'Gone to the hospital. Robert had a good night and is expected to be out of Intensive Care this morning. If all goes well, he'll be transferred to a hospital near home soon. His company has offered to fly them all back to Queensland, no charge.'

'Oh, that's great news,' she said, smiling.

'That's better,' he said, smiling back at her, and the comment had plainly been meant in warm approval of her smile.

Lori eyed him coolly. Who gave him the right to approve or disapprove of her morning demeanour? 'Now that Robert is out of danger, you'll be leaving, I expect. Back to your work with the film company.'

'I have someone covering for me,' he said, and though he smiled she thought he might not be entirely amused by her bluntness. 'And I have some business here with my publisher, so I'll stay on a few days. I need to let a few people know. Do you mind if I use your phone?'

'Of course not,' she said, and thought of him that night at the resort, talking on the phone to Justine while he waited to whisk her, Lori Tate, off to his bed for a little light diversion.

A few extra days? He could roll up his sleeping bag and find someone else's garden shed to sleep in. She got up, clattered a few plates and banged the dishwasher door closed. 'But you will pay for your calls, won't you? I may not be short of money, but I don't see why I should foot the bill for your long-distance small-talk with your girlfriend.'

He came to his feet, hands on hips, eyes narrowed. Lori wished she hadn't said that. It sounded petulant, even jealous. It wasn't, of course—how could it be? But the man was so full of himself, that that was how he would interpret it.

Silence for the count of six. Lori was exasperated. If only he would occasionally rush into speech without preparation, she might learn something to her advantage. 'Let me buy you dinner tonight,' he said smoothly. 'As some recompense for your hospitality to my family. I will pay for my phone calls as well, of course.'

She reddened, subtly reprimanded for her rudeness by his invitation. 'Thank you, that isn't necessary,' she said. 'Anyway, I have to go to an art show opening tonight.'

'Have dinner first. If you're late to an art show, it wouldn't matter.'

'It would, as it happens. This is Fairlie's exhibition—my cousin Carson's wife. She has nerves before an exhibition—always thinks no one will come. I promised to be there at the start.'

His smile was sardonic and she thought she had said too much, been too specific in her reasons for refusing him.

'And you always keep your promises,' he said softly.

Lori turned away and went to her bedroom to get ready for work. *Promises*... That superstitious feeling crept up on her again.

Her hair was vigorously brushed back and caught in a smooth knot at the nape. She applied her make-up in the usual two minutes. As she would go straight from the office to the art show, she wore a narrow-skirted black suit with a white blouse and put matching black crêpe trousers and a pink silk evening shirt into a protective zippered bag. Dark silk tights, plain black pumps. Lori slung a black bag over her shoulder.

She felt infinitely better about dealing with Haze now. As if she had zippered herself into a protective bag.

Haze was leaning against the bare-branched liquid-amber tree where the African lilies ran wild when she went to her car. Leaning there in the sun, reading the newspaper, he looked like one of those movie private eyes with someone under surveillance, trying to look inconspicuous. Except that he couldn't look inconspicuous if he tried.

'There's a picture of you in the paper—presenting that trophy yesterday,' he said.

'Is there?' she said with a grimace. 'I hate newspaper photos of myself.'

'They say the camera never lies,' Haze went on. 'I'd always thought that something of a joke.'

Until today. The unspoken words made her wince. She must look plainer than she usually did in newspaper pictures. Lori, long accustomed to not being beautiful, was momentarily depressed, and wished that the camera could have lied for her, just this once.

'Do you never wear your hair down?' he asked.

'Only on desert islands,' she said flippantly, then remembered that of course he didn't know about her uninhabited island. The man thought she'd somehow pulled strings to get a luxury suite at the resort without registering her name at the desk. It remained her private satisfaction that he knew less than he thought.

But he didn't pick up on the remark, merely stared at her. There was something different about the way he looked at her this time. As if he saw past the suit and the blouse and the dark silk tights. Not through them— not in that objectionable way that some men had of stripping a woman, any woman, with their eyes. It wasn't her unprotected body he was observing. It was *her*.

Lori faltered, more vulnerable than she'd ever felt at mere salaciousness. Without a word being spoken something had altered; she couldn't think what.

He followed her into the garage and opened the door of her car for her while she settled her spare clothes over the back seat. Lori got in, but he held onto the door when she would have closed it. He took a slip of paper from his pocket and gave it to her.

'What's this?'

'You can get me on that number on my mobile phone, should you need me,' he said. 'Any time.'

'I can't imagine why I would,' she said lightly. 'Unless I get stuck on a rock-face somewhere with a fraying rope.'

But she didn't want to make an issue of it and tucked the note into her wallet. He leaned in past her and laid the quartered, folded newspaper on the passenger seat beside her.

Lori pressed back in her seat but he paused before he withdrew, close enough for her to feel the warmth of his breath on her face. A faint trace of soap scent and coffee wafted to her nostrils. His short dark hair gleamed with life, and her eyes lingered on it as she remembered it longer, slipping forward to frame his face so that he looked like a blue-eyed Celtic warrior. She had tangled the strong, glossy length of it around her fingers, drawn him down to her...

'I could always grow it again,' he said provocatively.

'I don't like long hair on men,' she retorted, confirming the accuracy of his mind-reading.

He was brimming with confidence, blue eyes heavy-lidded, a sultry smile tilting his handsome mouth. 'You liked it.'

Relax. *Re*—breathe in—*lax*—breathe out. 'Please move out of the way, Haze. I have to go. And you will make other arrangements for the next few days, won't you? I don't care what you tell your sister, but if I find your things in my bedroom tonight I will throw them in the rubbish bin, I promise you.'

'I'll certainly make other arrangements, then,' he said, as if he were murmuring sweet nothings instead of accepting his marching orders. His gaze never left her mouth.

Heart racing, she said huskily, 'I don't think you're listening. I'm serious about it, Haze.'

His mouth touched hers briefly in a kiss so sweet, so tender that she felt certain she must be dreaming it. She wanted more, but raised her hand to his head too late and missed him. He smiled down at her arrested giveaway gesture, looked into her bemused eyes.

'I do take you seriously, Laura-love. I know you always keep your promises.'

The usual sarcasm had been missing from his voice when he'd said it that time. Lori was stationary at the corner set of traffic lights before she realised why.

A glance at the newspaper he had placed on the seat beside her showed her that he had folded it so that the photograph of her was on show. Usually, the newsprint faded out her hair, but her head was turned this time, as she handed the trophy to the girl and boy school captains. In profile she looked not bad at all, she thought critically, wondering if there was something about this picture that had put that disturbing look in Haze's eyes.

She looked as she always did at these kind of functions—slim and businesslike in her tailored clothes. Lori snatched up the newspaper for a closer look. Around her neck was Amanda's paperclip necklace, worn all day as she had promised.

'They say the camera never lies...' She smiled, pleased that he had not been commenting on her lack of dazzle, pleased that he now knew she had valued the promise made to a little girl. Yet she arrived at the Tate building in an introspective mood. It was only a paperclip necklace, but it was a chain of sorts—and she usually avoided chains like the plague.

# CHAPTER EIGHT

FAIRLIE'S art show was mounted on the ground floor of one of Melbourne city's splendid classic buildings, constructed in the euphoric, optimistic second half of the last century, when wool and wealth had been synonymous. The ornate architraves, carved wood and pedimented door and window-frames were a contrast in form for Fairlie's energetic contemporary paintings, the lofty ceilings and soaring stone columns of sympathetic proportions for her huge canvases. It was, Lori decided, the kind of setting that would favour her cousin Carson's proportions. Or Haze Callahan's.

Lori spied Fairlie in the distance, looking critically at a painting. A large pair of shoes was planted on the marble floor, visible beneath the display partitioning, which meant that Carson was already here. He was lucky to have Fairlie, but she was lucky to have him too. Carson would be a rock in times of need, and even the strongest woman could use a rock now and then.

Lori picked up a glass of wine from the tray of drinks on the unattended front table and made her way down the gallery. In deference to her nerves, Fairlie's closest family had come early. Lori said hello to David, Carson's son by his first marriage, who was setting up a camera on a tripod, then came across Fairlie's grandmother from Brisbane, holding the newest born Tate. Lori said hello to them too, and let the baby curl her tiny fingers around her thumb.

Babies and children and pregnant women were everywhere she went these days, she thought with a spasm of irritation.

Nan Holborn loyally supported Fairlie's modern paintings, but was wistfully representational in her own tastes. She was pointing out to the baby a 'little red puppy-dog' in the slashes of color of a canvas entitled *Archetype III*.

As she moved on Lori heard Fairlie's laughter. Carson was doing a good job of relaxing her. A large presence fell in step with her. It was Carson, resplendent in white shirt and dark trousers with braces. He was shrugging his bulky shoulders into a dinner jacket. 'Lori—I hardly recognised you with your hair loose,' he said.

Lori's mouth dropped open. She looked at the big feet under the canvas. 'I thought that was you over there,' she said, and even as she said it she registered that those feet were shod in stout leather crafted for walking in rough terrain. A terrible premonition seized her. She rounded the edge of the painting and saw just who was being so successful at soothing Fairlie's pre-exhibition nerves.

Only years of self-discipline stopped her spilling the wine from her glass. Carson swept his wife into his arms then urgently charged her to help him with the bow tie he produced from his pocket. For once he didn't have his wife's full attention. Fairlie was agog with curiosity. She rolled her eyes appreciatively from Haze to Lori before devoting herself to Carson's tie.

Lori stared at Haze. He wore drill trousers and a fawn T-shirt with numerous lines of words printed in darkest green. His hands were thrust into the pockets of his trousers, casually hooking back the edges of a heavy-duty black leather jacket. It had no padding and needed none but the substantial contours of his shoulders. Lori had a sudden vision of him as he'd looked on her island, standing at the bottom of the tree, his shoulders bare and brown and glistening in the sun.

'What are you doing here?' she whispered sharply, turning scarlet.

He smiled fondly at her. 'I see you took my advice.'
He reached out and touched the backs of his fingers to
her hair.

Now she wished she had not given in to the impulse
to loosen it. With dismay, she acknowledged that it had
been his comment that had made her do it. She batted
his hand away, alarmed that he had influenced her to
break a habit with nothing more than a passing
comment. It was only a hairdo and hardly mattered, but
it bothered her. Her hair today...what tomorrow? She
would not, *could* not achieve her goals if she started
changing herself to please a man...

'You weren't invited,' she said abruptly.

'I'm family.'

'You're not supposed to be here...that wasn't part
of the deal,' she said, trying to keep her eyes off him.
The lines of words on his T-shirt were instructions on
how to put out a fire properly before breaking camp.
'You're supposed to be a means to an end, that's all—
a convenient man in the background. Not getting mixed
up with my life, my home, my family...'

Haze took her arm, none too gently. She felt the bite
of his fingers in her flesh through the thin jacket and
the silk of her shirt. 'Store this in that computer of a
mind,' he said softly, bending to deliver the words directly into her ear. 'I will never be a convenient man.'

Lori would have pulled away, but was conscious of
being observed. Giving Haze his marching orders would
be considered assertive if she were a man, but she was
a woman and it would be described, with a wince, as
'making a scene in public'.

'I wanted to see you,' he said, propelling her to a space
alongside a giant potted stand of bamboo.

'What for? What could be so urgent?' she demanded,
and as she looked beyond him she saw a woman with
russet hair moving slowly between the pictures. Justine.
A chill breeze found her from out of nowhere. He was

here, of course, to meet Justine—and the only thing he could want to see Lori Tate about had to be connected.

'If it's a divorce you need,' she said coldly, because she had to give herself the advantage of mentioning it first, 'I agree entirely. Our deal has outlived its usefulness. I'll phone my solicitor first thing in the morning.'

His dark blue eyes blazed and his fingers flexed painfully on her arm. 'If you're going to behave like a thug—' she said between clenched teeth.

'You'll what?' He showed his own teeth, and she blinked at the sheer fury in him.

'I'll be forced to get the security guard to throw you out,' she said. Her eyes skated across his shoulders. 'The guard *and* Carson,' she amended, to make the threat at least feasible.

He smirked at the implied compliment, but his face fell when he looked up. 'Oh, hell!' he muttered, and then said a few other choice words before he looked searchingly at Lori.

'I've already seen her,' Lori said coolly. 'Why didn't you just say you were here to meet your gallery-owner friend? I suppose she's on a buying trip? Well, I can see The Uncles arriving and I have to circulate, so I'll leave you to it—'

But Haze wouldn't let her go. His arm went around her shoulders and she was caught in close to him, sheltered in the curve of his body. To have and to hold... What on earth was he doing?

'Hello, Justine,' he said, smiling. 'Fancy seeing you here. You've met Lori, my wife.'

The woman looked intently at Lori, then her eyes widened in recognition. 'Oh, yes. You were with Haze on the road that day, after he'd rescued Tony... I didn't realise *you* were the one.' Her gaze turned speculative as she studied them as a pair. 'It is a very peculiar marriage, if you don't mind me saying so.'

Haze grinned. 'I don't mind you saying so. Do you mind, Laura-love?'

'A very apt description,' Lori said briskly, attempting without success to withdraw her arm from his. Just what was he keeping up the pretence for? Her family knew their marriage was a fake, and the redhead knew that she, Justine, was the woman in possession.

Justine was even more beautiful than she remembered, if that were possible. Even the faint lines around her eyes were attractive, hinting that they'd been put there by singing and smiling. Her red hair was thick and glossy and cut by an expert to look as if a passionate lover had run his fingers through it just ten minutes ago. Jealously, Lori tried to think where Haze had been ten minutes ago. It took her a few moments to register that Justine was looking back at her with a thwarted intensity unexpected from the woman in possession.

Justine pouted at Haze. She wanted to know more about this peculiar marriage. How could they tolerate such long periods apart from each other? Where did they live in Melbourne? When Haze said he had moved into Lori's place, Justine flushed dark red.

'You wouldn't make that compromise for me,' she said under her breath.

She appeared to have a brief struggle with herself, and Lori felt a sudden desperate pity for her without quite understanding what was going on. Justine lingered long enough to redeem herself with some vivacious small talk about Tony and her gallery and the coincidence that the artist Fairlie Jones should turn out to be related to Haze by marriage. She made off as soon as was polite, her colour still high.

Lori watched in confusion as the redhead sought out Fairlie and pointed to a canvas. 'My wife.' The words resonated. Lori struggled with a new concept.

'That was stretching things a bit, wasn't it?' she said, to give herself time to think. 'Saying you'd moved in with me, when you slept in the garden shed last night.'

'You were with me in spirit in the garden shed,' he said soulfully. 'As I snuggled up by the hedge clippers and the garden shears I felt almost as if I had you there beside me.'

She laughed. 'She doesn't seem to know that we're not really married,' she said huskily. Haze looked down at her, his arm still close around her. His dark blue eyes were sombre.

'I didn't tell her.'

Lori couldn't look away now. She was hypnotised by his intensity. 'You didn't tell your family, you didn't tell your girlfriend...who *did* you tell?' she croaked.

'Nobody.' After a count of six, he added, 'She isn't my girlfriend. You jumped to conclusions about that.'

'I'd hardly call it jumping to conclusions when you practically *devoured* each other on the side of the road that day. And you *told* me that you and she had something going.'

'You asked me, if you remember, if I could deny that there'd ever been anything between us,' Haze said. 'And there had. Begun and finished months before. As for *devouring* each other,' he said, then paused, his gaze seeking out Justine's distant figure. His eyelids flickered and he looked rueful. 'Let's just say you might have got the wrong impression. Justine was distraught over Tony at the time.'

Lori took a mouthful of wine from her glass. 'So, everyone you know thinks you are *really* married?' she said. 'And now you'll have to explain why you're getting divorced. I can't understand why you've allowed that to happen.'

Haze touched her hair, watching his own movements. His gaze switched suddenly to hers. 'I know you can't,' he said, with irony.

He looked at her the way he had many times before, and the allure of it set her pulses racing. She could no longer cite Justine as good reason to resist it. Could no longer feel the sting to her pride the way she had that night in the resort restaurant, when she'd thought he'd wanted her as light entertainment before he went home to Justine. She felt like a fugitive, caught at last in the white searchlight, with no weapons, no defences.

'Relax, Laura-love,' he said wryly, seeing her tension. 'Remember I only married you for your money and you'll feel better.'

But she didn't feel better. Haze wandered off and she felt more confused than ever. A highly intelligent, capable woman with a fine education and years of experience in top level business should be able to work this out, she thought as she studied one of Fairlie's canvases without seeing a thing. But all her experience counted for very little where Haze was concerned.

'Wishful thinking' he'd said, when she'd asked him once before why he hadn't told his family their marriage was a fake. And he hadn't told Justine. Hadn't been seeing her, making love to her... Lori suppressed a rush of euphoria.

Fairlie's canvas was a vortex of greys lit and warmed from beneath by an underpainting of white and red. In the centre was a squiggle that was challenging Nan's powers of description. 'Now, look at this, Felicity, my little love,' she said, standing alongside Lori with the baby. 'This is a... oh, dear, I can't imagine... What do you think, Lori, my dear? It looks like something being dragged into a whirlpool.'

Lori felt a great empathy with that squiggle, at the mercy of the irresistible force of the vortex. 'Yes, just like that,' Lori said, and steeled herself as she saw Haze's path cross with that of The Uncles. Carson was there, performing introductions, and Lori breathed deep, oddly embarrassed and anxious. Anyone would think that she *cared* what they thought of the man she had married, she thought crossly.

There was some unsmiling scrutiny going on between the Tate males and Haze. If he thought he was going to get the warm welcome he'd had from Fairlie, Haze was very much mistaken, she thought with a shaft of spiteful satisfaction. And if he practised his lengthy pauses he wouldn't get a word in.

What overweening confidence, to turn up at an art gallery opening dressed as if he was about to set off on a three-day tramp in the mountains. He just didn't care. But The Uncles had rigid views on appropriate dress, as she had cause to know. For once, she found the thought quite pleasing.

She composed herself and spoke to her aunts, whose disapproving scrutiny of Haze's clothes was mingled with feminine admiration for the man himself. Aunt Cheryl's hair was tinted red and cut in a sad, youthful bob. She and the other aunts plied her with questions about this suddenly manifested husband, and Lori smiled serenely and marvelled that she could stand here like this, parrying their curiosity in a perfectly civilised way, while her mind jumped this way and that.

'Wishful thinking...' he'd said. Did he mean that he wanted their marriage to be real? Was that why he had arranged that idiotic wedding? So that it was more like a real one, not just for his family's benefit but for his own? Her heart pounded. Did he love her? Lori gave her empty glass to a passing waiter. He had no orange juice on his tray so she took another glass of wine, feeling the need to moisten her parched throat.

Love. Lori spilled a few drops of wine, brushed them from her black trousers. What a fool she was. What was she doing, speculating on whether he loved her or whether he wanted their marriage to be real, when love and marriage were not part of *her* plans? Which was why she had proposed marriage to him in the first place—

to stop herself getting involved in an affair that might have led somewhere she didn't want to go.

Lori blinked, aware of certain flaws in her logic. In distaste, she decided she was behaving badly, self-indulgently in dwelling on possibilities she had no intention of realising. She had no right to wonder if he loved her when she knew she couldn't afford to love him. No right to pounding heartbeats and trembling hands. She had some more wine and felt she had got things into proper perspective again.

And yet...

Her eyes kept seeking him out. Her ears kept straining for the sound of his voice, as if she were a receiver tuned to a radio frequency. But Haze seemed to be listening, rather than talking. It was, she supposed, a survival tactic in hostile territory.

Tangled scraps of conversation reached her.

'Haze—funny name. Parents come up with some funny...'

'Now, my little... this is a lovely picture of a...'

'Clark—Errol—'

'Where are the red SOLD stickers?'

'We had another brother—Lorelei's father, Tyrone.'

'The parents were keen moviegoers, you see. Could have been worse, of course...'

'...sold three paintings already! *Three*, Carson!'

'A gee-gee—a big horsie in your mummy's painting, see?'

'Could have called one of us Rock...'

It dawned on Lori that the unsmiling scrutiny had turned to tentative friendliness. A gust of masculine laughter echoed up to the coffered ceiling. Uncle Clark slapped Haze on the back. Even Mark was smiling. Haze seemed to be having no trouble at all with his pauses. Everyone waited attentively through them until he uttered. Lori swigged down some more wine, forgetting her rule of abstinence made because wine always made her sleep. Tonight it was making her pugnacious.

Mark sought her out and said, 'Just met your husband.' And he looked at her with respect. Because she was attached to a man he thought was impressive. *Respect!* When she had worked so hard for so long to earn his respect—studied, disciplined herself, sacrificed her leisure and private life. She had dreamed of having respect from all of them, but for her efforts, for her sheer dedication, not for managing to nab a man who had earned their respect in a matter of minutes.

'And did you find out what kind of a wimp marries a woman for her money, then?' she said. 'Did you notice if he's wearing his *leash*?'

Mark was sheepish at the reminder of his spiteful comments.

'I was out of line there. Sorry. Put it down to disappointment at losing Woody's place,' he said, and added plaintively, 'Just for a while there I thought I was the favoured one... I mean, she could have left it to us both, couldn't she? But I was only ever Woody's second choice.'

Lori put a hand on her brother's arm. 'Oh, that's ridiculous, Mark.'

'Is it?' He gave a wry grin. 'It's not easy, having a brilliant little sister dogging your footsteps.'

She stared in astonishment. 'Brilliant?'

'For God's sake, you hardly ever put a foot wrong. Even when you get a man out of the grab-bag just for legal purposes you don't get some nerd—you get a man like Callahan.' He pulled a face. 'He's a hit. You know how The Uncles revere someone who's stood up to them and won. Play your cards right and they'll probably offer him a seat on the board one of these days.'

He went off and Lori clenched her wine glass, torn between glee that Haze had thrown all their preconceptions into a cocked hat and fury that he had done it so

effortlessly. A seat on the board? That was an exagger-
ation, of course. Nevertheless ... She scowled at The
Uncles as they came up to her singly and praised her for
finding such an outstanding man.

'Yes, he must be outstanding,' she snapped to Clark.
'He took you to court and beat you, didn't he?'

Accustomed to her cool composure, Uncle Clark
stared. 'Are you feeling all right, Lorelei?' he asked, and
the quite genuine note of concern annoyed her more than
ever.

'For heaven's sake, don't call me Lorelei. I *hate* being
called Lorelei. Call me Lori.'

Smiling, Clark patted her on the shoulder. 'I can't
promise anything. It's hard to break the habit of a
lifetime.'

Lori pushed her face close to his. 'Well, *try*, Uncle.
And there's another habit you should try to break soon.
Aunt Cheryl is starting to wear her hair like the twenty-
year-olds you run around with. Isn't it time you both
grew up?'

He turned puce and moved away. At this rate, Lori
thought, tossing back another mouthful of wine, no one
on the board would be speaking to her. She didn't care.
She looked around and beckoned the waiter, but a large,
solid body casually inserted itself between her and the
approaching drinks tray.

'Oh, if it isn't Indiana Jones,' she said, waggling her
hand to wave him aside so that she could get at the
drinks. Haze failed to understand her semaphore and
took her arm, moving her slowly but irrevocably past
the exhibits to a side room where Carson's day suit lay
crumpled across a bench and an electric jug and sundry
cups and jars of coffee cluttered a sink.

'Sit down,' Haze said. 'I'll make some coffee.'

Lori stiffened. He hadn't misunderstood her semaphore at all. 'You are not, I hope, insinuating that I've
had too much to drink?'

'I never insinuate.' Haze pushed aside Carson's clothes and thrust her onto the bench. 'You've had too much to drink,' he said bluntly. 'What you need is a cup of coffee.'

'What you need...' Lori leaped up again, her temper blazing. 'How dare you monitor me! By what right do you assume to tell me what I need?'

'If you have any more you may say or do something you'll regret.' He went over to the sink and filled the kettle.

'You—patronising, pompous—!' she shouted, hands on hips. 'I'm a grown woman, and if I make a mess of things it's my own mess and I will deal with it. I don't need you or anybody making decisions for me, do you hear?'

He winced. 'I should think everyone can hear,' he said drily.

Lori paced. 'Who do you think you are... removing me from temptation like some silly little girl, in front of everyone? I have spent too long and worked too hard on my credibility to have it undermined by a—an overgrown lout who turns up at an art gallery opening dressed for an expedition into the interior!'

'I think getting pickled would damage your credibility more than this overgrown lout.' He smiled as he spooned instant coffee into a mug. *Smiled*.

Lori was beside herself. He didn't have a clue. He thought it was amusing! 'That's *my* decision,' she snapped. 'You weren't invited, Haze. Why don't you leave?'

'No, no—couldn't do that. The Uncles would be disappointed,' he said aggravatingly. 'Funny thing, after all the bad blood between us—they seem to like me.'

'Oh, yes,' she said, bitterly reflecting on the mysterious basis of male mateship. 'And *respect* you. Wonderful, isn't it? I arrived at Tate's uninvited too. But I came fully qualified and I worked my—my rear off to fit in. I've taught myself to keep cool, to let all their damned patronising remarks pass! I've taught myself not to cry or show any temper! I'm good at what I do—very good.

'And,' she said, with a scathing look at his T-shirt, 'I have always made sure I turned up wearing the right clothes for the right occasion—and do I earn their respect?' She flung away, paced the length of the room and back again, her black jacket flapping in agitation. 'You walk in here with a lousy reputation as a gold-digger, wearing your old boots and a gross T-shirt with *campfire* tips on it... but you're a man, and they give you the benefit of the doubt, and in less than half an hour they're giving you the good old back-slapping ritual—treating you like you belong!'

Her throat closed over, choking any further words, and she turned away, hastily flicking her knuckles over her eyes. Haze took her shoulders and turned her to face him. 'Dammit,' she muttered with a shaky laugh, embarrassed by the tears on her cheeks. 'I'll have to work harder on the crying bit.'

He pulled her into him and briefly she leaned her forehead on his shoulder. Lori thought how ridiculous it was that the cause of her upheaval could be such a comfort. Her eyes opened, inches from his chest. '...sure to douse the flames of your campfire', his T-shirt preached.

He dug in a pocket and brought out a handkerchief which he thrust into her hand. Lori took it gratefully and stepped back to use it. Watching her, he put his hands on his hips and the black jacket parted to convey more advice. 'Check that no spark remains to start another fire...' Lori did her deep breathing routine... *re*—breathe in—*lax*—breathe out. At last she had herself in hand. She took her jacket edges in both hands, gave a quick tug.

Haze look sardonic. 'Back to business?' he said.

'As I was saying earlier,' she said, as if he hadn't spoken, 'we need to wind this whole thing up. I'll arrange for my solicitor to draw up divorce papers. Should she send them to your office or home address?'

'Do you think a few legal papers will finish it?'

'That's all that's required to end a marriage.'

'I'm not talking about a marriage,' he said irritably. 'We haven't got a *marriage*, so ending it means nothing. But we do have some—unresolved tension. What are we going to do about it, Laura-love?' He caught her arm, drew her close.

'Divorce papers won't finish it,' he said softly, his eyes on her mouth. 'We'll always wonder what it would have been like to be lovers... because that's what we should have been—what we would have been right from the start if you'd followed your instincts for pleasure instead of marching back to your penthouse, or wherever, to put together a business deal. Your architecturally—' he bent and touched his mouth to her neck with each following word '—symmetrical—business—plan.'

Lori shivered.

'We should have that affair now,' Haze went on, sliding his hands under her jacket, up her back, and she felt the heat of his hands scarcely diminished by the thin layer of silk between her flesh and his. He angled his head and kissed beneath her jaw. 'And keep on having it until it just fades out naturally...'

Till death us do part, she thought, torn between old goals and new temptations. Her hands slipped up over his arms as if possessed of their own goals. She wondered how long it would take to just fade out naturally for Haze... a week, two? Six months? Common sense told her this was stupid, that any dilution of a nice, clean ending to their deal would only lead to trouble.

'Haze—' she began.

A low laugh came from the doorway. Fairlie said, 'Don't let me stop you—I know how it is.'

'No, actually, it isn't,' Lori said, moving out of range of all that temptation and fruitless advice on how to put out fires safely.

'Boy, I'm beginning to think things must have got crowded in that two-man tent,' Fairlie teased. 'Still, I suppose you're used to tents, considering the business you're in,' she said to Haze.

'Tent?' Haze said, eyes narrowed. He was quick on the uptake, but Lori could see he was having trouble with this concept.

Fairlie signalled that she was coming in response to a call from the gallery. 'My environmental research friend said to tell you thanks for the notes and to let him know when you want another desert island holiday. You can water his plants any time.' She laughed and hurried away to her guests.

'Water his plants?' Haze said sardonically. His arms were crossed over his chest. Body language experts claimed that the pose was a defensive one, but Lori was darned if she could see it. He looked puzzled but formidable. 'What tent?'

She smiled, pleased to be able to tell him how wrong he had been. 'I stayed in a tent on the island. It belongs to a university research department.' She waved a casual hand. 'I watered some experimental plants, checked precipitation and made some notes in exchange for the use of the campsite.'

His eyes flickered as he made the various adjustments to his assumptions. 'You—stayed in a tent. *Slept* in a tent?'

'Yes,' she said, eyeing him maliciously. 'You have no idea how dark it can be away from the bright lights...the ground is hard, the wilderness is full of rustling, unseen things.'

He smiled ruefully, hearing an echo of his own words. 'How could I know? You didn't look the type.'

Lori laughed. 'I change my business suit for a frilly dress and suddenly you treat me like a dizzy little girl. How naïve can you get?'

'I don't recall doing that,' he said, studying her with a disturbing intensity that seemed to have nothing to do with the current exchange.

'"The tropics gone to your head, have they?"' She mimicked his indulgent tone. '"You wouldn't sleep a wink, Laura, my sweet." Well, I'm willing to admit to the odd moment of apprehension in the dark, but I managed rather well.'

There was definitely admiration in his eyes. Lori was pleased to see it, but annoyed as well. The great master of the outdoors was impressed, was he, by a woman who could rough it without whining? 'You're an unusual woman,' he said.

Lori laughed. 'I know. You let the trembling green dress lead you astray.'

'Here I was, thinking you had pulled strings to stay in some secluded little luxury hide-out at the resort, away from the tourist masses.'

She felt the effect of the wine in her head, heard herself laugh again. It was heady enough, seeing Haze surprised and admiring.

'I imagined you slipping away from me that night to go to your luxurious apartment and work out your famous deal,' he said musingly. 'Instead—what did you do?'

She walked out into the gallery again, enjoying this. 'I changed on the beach and waited for the tide to turn. Then I waded across the channel and went back to my camp.'

'How long did you have to wait on the beach?'

'Oh, an hour and a half.'

He gave a low whistle. 'Uncomfortable?'

'Not the greatest.'

'It must have been dark—wading across the coral—bare-footed?'

She wrinkled her nose. 'Hmm. It was a bit of a worry. Didn't know what I was putting my feet on in the dark. I fell and ended up soaked, of course,' she said airily, to show that she could take adversity in her stride. 'But I expected that.'

'And then you had to get to your camp... where was it? Inland? Through the bush? At night.'

It was something he had doubtless done himself many times, and she was both pleased and ruffled by the surprise in his voice. Patronising devil, she thought.

'Yes, inland. A good ten minutes in the dark, even with a torch. I don't know why you're so surprised. If you hadn't been so patronising before, you might have got to see it.'

His eyes narrowed. 'I don't follow.'

'"You're not the type to rough it in the woods,"' she mimicked. 'I was going to invite you to my camp until you came over all superior and treated me like a pampered little girl.'

The sudden flare of triumph in his eyes made her backtrack. What had she said to give him that conquering look? I was going to invite you to my camp... So what?

'"It would be wonderful to sleep out under the stars..."' Haze said softly. 'Were you working your way up to invite me to share the wilderness with you?'

Too late, Lori saw the trap. In pursuit of a petty victory she had left herself wide open.

'Lori Tate—the solo crossworder, the marathon runner, wonderwoman... You were thinking of asking me into your tent, way back then?'

She felt the rush of blood and alcohol to her head. A slight giddiness made her sway. Haze was too sharp, too intelligent not to see the significance of it. She hadn't truly seen it herself until later, when she'd known he was talking on the phone to Justine.

Absolutely alone, she'd told him she would be on her holiday—just the way she liked it. And she'd meant it at the time. But just days later she would have let him in. Her only comfort since then had been that he hadn't a clue about it. She felt she'd lost a layer of protective clothing.

'Must have been the champagne,' she said, managing a careless wave of a hand. She drank from her wine glass. Hair of the dog, she thought. Was that a good idea?

'What *really* made you run away that night?' he asked.

She gripped her glass tightly. Run away? Why hadn't she kept her mouth shut? She had only just got away with her daft story about a cool, considered choice of business over pleasure because of her reputation, and because he had pictured her retiring purposefully to her luxury apartment to work out the details of her deal. A journey by torchlight, wading through reef rockpools in the dark, plunging through the bush to a tent on a deserted island in preference to spending the night in comfort with him, had all the hallmarks of panicked flight.

Lori was temporarily at a loss. He wanted an affair and that was all. Now he knew that she, who shied away from intimacy, had been ready to commit herself at the start, she felt vulnerable. Haze was clearly the one with the lesser investment in this relationship, the one with least to lose. No wonder he had that smoky, confident look of the conqueror about him. There was a constricted feeling in her chest. She took a long draft of wine to give herself time to think.

He reached for her hand, drew the glass away from her mouth.

'Laura-love, you really have had enough.'

# CHAPTER NINE

HE HAD not spoken loudly, but loud enough for Clark Tate to hear. Her uncle looked over, smirking with approval at the sight of the independent Lori Tate being brought into line by her husband. It would be all over Tate's in no time: 'He'll stand no nonsense' and 'She's met her match' and various other self-satisfied male observations which would enhance Haze's image and diminish hers.

She flushed deeply. Her eyes blazed. She wrenched free, splashing wine on his leather jacket and the floor. 'Why don't you...?' she snapped, and left him standing there.

He was nowhere to be seen when she decided to leave a short time after. 'You're not driving home in that state,' Carson said when she made her farewells. He took her elbow in a bossy grip and her temper soared.

'For heaven's sake,' she hissed, shaking him off. 'If one more overbearing, patronising man tells me what I should or shouldn't do, I will scream.'

Carson studied her with some of his old dislike. Fairlie said anxiously, 'At least let us phone for a taxi for you.'

'I have a mobile phone,' Lori said, forming the words with dignified deliberation. 'I have been phoning for cabs for myself for *years*. Why is everyone suddenly acting as if I can't make simple decisions for myself?'

She made her exit. She knew why. It was because there was a big, strong man on the scene. That was why she had to make her way alone, because as soon as there was a big, strong man on the scene a woman somehow was seen as weaker, indecisive, flighty. She strode out, her temper not cooled by the sharp breeze that spat out a few drops of rain. So when she turned the corner and came upon a teenaged girl struggling to throw off the grip of a burly young man, Lori didn't wait to ask herself if it was any of her business.

'Are you OK?' she said to the girl, who was delicate, flower-faced, with long, curling dark hair and a crushed-strawberry mouth. The man turned and snarled at Lori, but she stared back at him, her accumulated fury bolstering her against the impression of bad temper backed up by a hefty frame.

'Get lost!' he said.

'Is this man harassing you?' Lori went on, ignoring him to speak to the girl.

'I *said* get lost!' he shouted, red-faced.

'I'm not talking to you,' Lori said levelly. 'But to this young woman.'

'Yeah, well, she doesn't want to talk to you, so push off!'

'I have a mobile phone,' Lori said to the girl. She pulled the phone from her bag. 'Do you want me to call the police?'

The man let go of the girl and advanced on Lori. He grabbed her wrist. 'I've had it up to here with interfering bloody women!' he said between clenched teeth. 'First, her mother and now the Lone Ranger with her mobile phone. Give me that!' He made a snatch at the phone. Lori chopped her hand down on his forearm and he bleated with the pain of it.

Everything happened at once. Large, stinging drops of rain fell. A taxi cruised alongside. Invective poured from the crushed-strawberry mouth of the flower-faced girl. She pummelled Lori, got a grip on her hair and pulled. Lori yelped and staggered. The phone went flying as she threw up her hand to protect herself. The man who had been threatening her a moment ago was now her champion, holding the virago off her. The rain pelted

down. Lori backed off to find the phone and slipped on
the wet pavement. The girl kicked her on the ankle.

'Serves you right for sticking your nose in where it
doesn't belong!'

'Now, ladies—is he worth fighting over?' said a new
voice.

Lori, sprawled on the pavement, her face crumpled in
pain, saw two uniformed men through the rats' tails of
her wet hair. It wasn't a taxi that had pulled up alongside,
but a police patrol car.

'Thank goodness,' she said. But as she scrambled up
one of the officers grabbed her arm and hoisted her to
her feet, pushed her to the car.

'We'll sort this out at the station,' the officer said.

Horrified, Lori resisted. 'Look, I can explain. These
two were fighting and I was just passing—'

'Yeah, right. In the car.'

She almost stamped her foot. Eyeing him coldly, she
said, 'You are making a big mistake. It must be quite
obvious that I am not the type to get involved in un-
dignified tussles in the street.'

He looked her over. 'Yeah, right,' he said again. She
was wet, her clothes were dirty from her fall on the
pavement and her ankle was bleeding. And there was a
run in her tights. Lori found that more aggravating than
anything else.

In the car, Lori remained silent while the other two
bickered and accused each other until they remembered
they had a common enemy and accused Lori instead.
When they got to the station, she decided, she would
simply show her identification and that would be that.
Once they knew she was Lorelei Tate she would get an
apology, some coffee and a car to take her home.

But at the station she recognised a newspaperman
mooching about looking for story-leads on a slow night.
Horrified, she imagined the glee of the Press. TATE DI-
RECTOR IN BRAWL. IS THERE ANYTHING THIS LITTLE

GAL WON'T DO? And the pictures. The reporter had a
camera. She dropped her head so that her soaked hair
hung in concealing strings. She would never live it down.
Never.

'Name?' an officer asked.

She hesitated. 'Callahan,' she said. 'Mrs Haze
Callahan.'

When the duty officer leaned forward, sniffed, then
asked if she'd been drinking, she admitted shamefacedly
that she had. 'Sorry,' she said, keeping her tone humble
so as not to attract any attention. She bit her lip when
the officer asked if her husband knew she was out alone
on a night like this, getting involved in unsavoury goings-
on.

'He'll kill me,' she said, raising imploring eyes to him.
'You won't charge me with anything, will you? Please?'

The man was magnanimous. Smiling at this very
proper reaction, he said he couldn't just let her walk out
in the state she was in, and the worse for drink as well.
'You get someone to come and pick you up and we'll
let you off with a warning. If you take my advice you'll
ring your husband now and tell him the whole thing.
But some other responsible person will do if you can't
face the music, OK?'

She gritted her teeth when he patted her shoulder.
Caught between the devil and the deep blue sea. She
couldn't call anyone from the family. They were probably
all still at Fairlie's exhibition, anyway. Lori felt a surge
of self-pity and wished she, too, were there. She fished
around in her wallet and withdrew a card. With a shaking
hand she pressed the number scrawled on the back. Mrs
Haze Callahan. The first time she had ever said it out
loud. She murmured it again to herself, absently, like a
child repeating a new word. The number rang.

'Callahan,' he said.

She closed her eyes, let go of a breath. Earlier she had
thought knowing Haze was like being drawn into one of

Fairlie's vortices. Now the sound of his voice was a link with sanity, with warmth and feeling and life itself.

'Haze, it's Lori,' she said huskily. What she had intended to say was something like, Would you mind coming to the police station? Or, I'd like to ask a favour. But, because she was prey to this extraordinary welling of feeling, what she said was, 'I need you.'

There was a silence too long even for him, and she thought for a moment that the mobile phone connection had been severed because of the storm. Somehow, though, she knew he was still there. *Felt* him still there, on the end of the line. 'Haze...' she said, already retreating from the intensity of the bald statement that had silenced him. 'I'm—um—kind of stuck on a rockface with a frayed rope.'

He gave a snort of laughter. 'Where are you?'

She grimaced when she told him, but the man who rescued crazy adolescents off cliff-faces before breakfast didn't miss a beat. 'I'm on my way,' he said.

Half an hour later he walked through the door, a big man, shoulders tense, eyes swiftly searching for her. He must be wondering what he would find. His hair was mussed and glistening with raindrops. There were drops on the shoulders of his jacket too, and she choked back a hysterical laugh, thinking that it was a good job it was leather, what with all this moisture about. First wine, then rain... Lori got to her feet, but he didn't see her right away.

'My name is Callahan,' he told the duty officer.

The man nodded. 'Right—your wife's ready to go. No charges.'

Haze blinked several times. 'My wife?'

He saw Lori and took in her bedraggled state, only partially improved by the use of a comb. She came up to him and tried to look the errant, remorseful wife. 'Thanks for coming so soon, darling.'

His eyes narrowed at the endearment, but he caught her around the waist and said, 'What have you been doing this time, honey?'

The sergeant shook his head at the implication that she was a persistent offender. 'Don't let us see you back here, Mrs Callahan. I'd go easy on the drink, if I were you. You know women have a lower alcohol tolerance than men.' He threw a conspiratorial look at Haze, as if to say, She needs a stern but gentle hand.

Lori sent Haze a look that warned him not to say, I told you so. But those dark blue eyes, warmed with amusement and more besides, quite undid her. She flushed and involuntarily lifted a hand to her bedraggled hair in the universal feminine gesture.

'Off you go, then,' said the sergeant indulgently, as if she were a twelve-year-old.

Lori nearly giggled. 'Thanks for being so understanding, Sergeant Reynolds.' She glimpsed sheer astonishment in Haze's eyes. The reporter, pacing about, dictating into his mobile phone, turned in their direction, and Lori pressed her face into Haze's shoulder. The smell of damp leather filled her nostrils. After a moment of rock-like stillness, he put his arms around her.

A mighty sob broke from her, one that had been a lifetime in the forming. Standing in a police station under harsh fluorescent lights, Lori felt a rush of emotion and a certainty that this man mattered to her—that she had been running and running and now she was tired of it. Something meaningful had happened inside herself. She didn't quite know what, but she knew nothing would be the same again.

'Take me home,' she said, her mouth forming the words against his neck. And it wasn't for Sergeant Reynolds' benefit this time.

\*     \*     \*

The rain slanted down. Wet pavements glistened, stained with the colours of neon lights—red, blue, emerald. The night air smelled of the damped-down dust of the city, the sharp tang of petrol and exhaust fumes, the earthiness of wet soil and street trees. The sound of tyres on the wet road was a loud whisper.

He had a taxi waiting. They got in; Haze gave her address, and as the vehicle moved away he looked at her and said, 'Mrs Callahan?'

She knew what he was asking. 'Yes.'

In the strobe effects of the streetlights his eyes glittered, nostrils flared. He took her hand, stroked at her wrist with his thumb. 'Cold hands, warm heart.'

Rain pelted down as they let themselves into the house. The house was quiet, but there was a light on in Jackie's room.

'Quick,' Haze said, whisking Lori into the bathroom. 'This is one time I do not want to make conversation with my sister.' He switched on the heater, shrugged off his leather jacket then turned to her, slipped his hands beneath the lapels of her jacket. 'I know this sounds corny, but let me help you out of those wet clothes.'

She laughed and immediately quelled the sound, conscious of his sister down the corridor. His assistance was satisfyingly unhurried. He removed her jacket and unfastened the buttons of her pink silk shirt, tending every new glimpse of skin with slow, sliding kisses. He unclipped her bra and removed it in agonising slow motion, caressed the upper curves of her breasts, the sides, the valley between, until he came at last to the centers. And the thrill of anticipation was pale compared to the sensation of his suckling mouth.

'Oh, yes,' she heard herself whisper. The bathroom acoustics made the word echo. 'Yes...yes...yes...'

When Lori made to unbuckle his belt, he pushed her hands away. 'Not yet, Laura-love. I've been waiting too

long for this and I'm on a short fuse. I don't want a
premature celebration.'

She stifled a giggle again, but Haze was inching down
her trousers and her undies with them, and his attention
to detail rendered her breathless. Naked, she rubbed
against him and he groaned, pushed her away and
reached past her to turn on the shower. As steam began
to rise he nudged her into the glassed cubicle, and,
without taking his eyes off her, bent to remove his boots
and socks. He unbuckled his belt, unzipped his trousers.

Lori could wait no longer. She hooked her fingers into
his waistband and drew him under the cascading water.
Instantly his T-shirt was soaked, semi-transparent and
stuck to his beautiful body. Lori laughed softly as the
drenched instructions for safely putting out fires rumpled
upwards under her urgent hands. Drops of water hit his
belt buckle and set up a faint tinkling sound. The T-shirt
fell soggily to the tiled floor and Lori put her hand over
her mouth to quell her laughter as Haze muttered and
cursed and shimmied to remove his drill trousers.

'I think they've shrunk,' he complained, then, with a
wicked gleam in his eyes, 'But nothing else has.'

It was no idle boast. He grinned at her small sound
of appreciation as he stood naked at last, his superb
musculature sheened with coursing water. But when he
pulled her close he gave a ragged sigh and held her tight
for long moments, as if to take an imprint—body upon
body. Lori kissed his shoulders, his neck, and, when he
lifted her, wrapped her legs around him. So close, so
tantalisingly close.

His eyes were heavy, glittering, his breathing uneven.

'I don't think you can have been working nearly as
hard as you claim,' he said.

His large hands applied a little pressure on her
backside, tilted her more evocatively against him, and
Lori was distracted with the immediate possibilities.
'What?' she croaked.

'You definitely have not worked your rear off,' he said.

Lori laughed, loving him more every moment, this sexy, earthy, powerful, tender man, who made her laugh while he made her want as she'd never wanted before. Mist rose around them, the water rained down on them, and somehow she was sure she could hear bells. 'Haze,' she murmured, moving her hips.

For a long moment he held her there. Lori felt his heat, smelled his skin, ran fingertips over the bunched arm muscles that supported his weight. She shifted impatiently, slid her hands down to his flanks and wrapped her legs tighter around him, dragging in her breath audibly at the poised, controlled strength of him.

'Please,' she whispered and, as if he had been waiting for an invitation to cross the threshold, he gathered her closer in strong arms and came inside.

'Do you think Jackie will notice there was only one shower?' Lori said much later as they lay in bed. They had dozed, talked, and drunk hot chocolate made furtively in the kitchen lest Jackie hear them and come out for a midnight chat before they could escape again to the bedroom.

'If that's all she heard, we should be thankful.'

Lori laughed, still too euphoric to be embarrassed by the recollection of her own echoing cries at her climax. Her body glowed still, and she felt a sharp pang of renewed desire as she tried to recapture the exact sensation of Haze inside her.

'I want to...' She drew an index finger down his magnificent body, her eyes following her own exploratory path over muscle and skin—smooth as silk and rough with hair. With an arm behind his head, Haze watched her too, and made a hoarse sound as her hand skimmed over him. He shivered and his body clenched, and she felt a wild elation at her own power. 'But my hands are cold,' she said in mock sadness, holding her hands away from him.

His eyes were heavy-lidded, his cheeks flushed. 'Then warm them, Laura-love,' he said.

'Mightn't that be...um...a bit deflating?' she asked.

'What goes down can always go up again,' he said. His frankness sent her brows up and colour to her cheeks, and he laughed softly, complacently.

'You're very sure of yourself,' she murmured.

'Cocksure.'

'I am going to wipe the smile off your face,' she told him, and she took him in her cold hands. He let out a shout and arched his back off the bed. 'Lie back and think of the Bank of England,' she said, smiling as she trailed her mouth over the ridged muscle of his midriff.

Presently, when her hands were warm and the smile was still on his face, he surged up from the bed and tumbled her onto her back. Then there was one of Haze's most enjoyable pauses, while she imagined the delights to come, and in a little while a feeling of wild elation that her imaginings were poor things compared to reality.

She woke for no good reason and lay listening to the sound of Haze's breathing. Some pale light filtered through the slatted blinds and looped muslin curtains and found its way onto the bed. Lori pushed herself up on one elbow and looked at him, engrossed in the lines of his face and the grain of his skin, and it could have been a minute, or five, or ten before she noticed that his eyes were open.

'Mmm. Morning,' he mumbled, pressing his mouth to her neck.

The phone rang, an alien sound in this silvery, dawn-lit place. Lori turned a little in her habitual movement to pick it up, for it was right beside her, and there were only inches between her hand and the receiver when Haze lunged across her, planting his big body squarely over hers. His hand closed over the receiver. Looking down at her, he said, 'Callahan,' then, 'Hello? Hello—?' and then he hung up. 'Nobody there. Must have been a wrong number,' he said easily.

'I wish you hadn't done that,' Lori said crossly. 'It is my phone after all, and I can't imagine what people will think to hear you answer it at five in the morning.'

'They'll imagine you're in bed with me,' he said. 'And they'll be right. So what?'

So what, indeed? Lori found, on reflection, that she cared less for what people might think than for Haze's too ready dismissal of her own concern about it. 'I'm perfectly accustomed to answering my own phone at all hours. I'd prefer you didn't dive across and land like a dead weight on me if it rings again.'

'Not a *dead* weight, Laura-love, surely?' he said, the words muffled into her neck. He gave a wicked thrust to let her know just how alive he was. 'And this morning, Laura-love,' he said, his voice husky with promise, 'I'm on a ve—ry long fuse.'

It was after seven before Lori dreamily surfaced. She looked at the clock consideringly for several seconds before its significance became clear. 'Seven-fifteen,' she wailed, and leapt to her feet. 'I've got an early appointment.'

With dismay she looked at the disorganisation of her bedroom. Her discarded clothes, which had been flung off with lover-like impatience in the bathroom last night, were mere untidiness now. His trousers and shirt were in the dryer, but his shoes and socks lay on the floor. Red-faced, she hurried around, gathering up the evidence of last night's passion, aware of a tiny spurt of irritation.

Normally she chose her business outfit the night before—pressed skirts that needed pressing, polished her shoes, checked her tights. Today she was not only late waking but had made no preparations. She had no time for a morning run, no time for breakfast.

Hastily, she flung open her wardrobe door and took out a grey suit and blue shirt. Wrapping herself in a housecoat, she dashed out to turn on the iron to heat while she quickly polished black pumps and took out the matching leather bag to pack with her daily kit of make-up, spare tights and the emergency articles that a woman had to carry 'just in case'.

And all the time she was aware of Haze, his head propped up on one muscular forearm, watching her. She looked over and smiled at him every so often as she hurried to the laundry to press her skirt, hurried back and then out again to the shower.

'It's a terrible waste,' he said.

Lori met his eyes in the mirror as she brushed back her hair and snapped on a band. 'What is?'

'The beautiful body of an athlete, hidden in grey flannel.'

She smiled, warmed by his admiration. But she was conscious of annoyance too. 'I could say the same. Such a waste, hiding such a beautiful body under those awful T-shirts you wear, those baggy army fatigues.'

He showed his teeth and half sat up, bringing both arms behind his head in a pose that dramatically highlighted his amazing shoulders and centurion chest. The vain devil. He knew he was stunning, compelling. After last night he knew exactly how stunning she found him because she had told him—repeatedly. And shown him. Also repeatedly. *And* this morning.

Lori swallowed, averted her eyes and jabbed in some hairpins to secure her hair in a knot. Everyone said that the morning after was a problem. But she hadn't anticipated this puzzling blend of awkwardness, shyness, excitement and vexation. Nothing would be the same again, she had thought. She had been right. This morning nothing was the same.

Her body felt super-sensitive, as if she'd acquired more nerve-endings during the night. Her thoughts were chaotic, and illustrated with explicit visuals with lots of bronze flesh tones and sooty black and darkest navy blue. Her bedroom was chaotic too—the dressing table strewn with foreign objects that Haze had tossed there last night. His wallet, phone, credit cards, bunch of keys, notebook, loose change. His boots had fallen on the floor, not in some vulnerable arrangement, pigeon-toed or on their side, but parallel, planted as firmly and immovably as if their owner were in them.

And the man himself was in her bed, dwarfing the embroidered cushions he had stuffed behind him, his imposing size and physique rendering the pastel florals of her bedlinen almost invisible.

Her irritation grew and she moved purposefully around the room, sweeping up his sundry belongings into a small pile on the dressing table, pushing his boots to attention in a corner. As she automatically straightened the clock and the lamp on her bedside table Haze stretched across the bed and clamped a hand around her wrist.

'It's no good, Laura-love,' he said softly. 'You can't put things back the way they were.'

'What?' she said.

'I get the feeling that I'm being classed with the clothes on the floor and the loose change on the dresser. A nuisance, messing up your nice, tidy bedroom.' He looked up at her and she saw the steely look in his eyes. 'Your nice, tidy life.'

'No,' she said, but she flushed. 'I'm just not used...to sharing my space, that's all. I—never have.'

His eyebrows went up. 'Never? You've never lived with a lover—not ever?'

Lori pulled against his grip, but he wasn't to be shifted.

'For heaven's sake, you make it sound like my lovers have been legion,' she said crossly. 'I've been out with a few men, but there was only one lover...'

He frowned. 'Carl? Or the guy that had the accident?'

'It was over between us some months before he—it happened. We never lived together. And Carl—' She wrinkled her nose. 'I let you think he was a boyfriend; I don't know why. He worked at Tate's for a while, that was all. I hardly knew the man.'

His eyes glittered. He gave a careless tug and she tumbled onto the bed, on top of him and the crumpled floral sheets.

'Haze—what are you—?'

With a lithe twist he had her on her back, and was leaning over her, pinning one of her wrists to the bed. The sheets slid away to remind her that he was naked. 'Just so that I make myself clear,' he said, staring down at her, 'don't think of me as a tame lover, content to be invited in now and then when you can be bothered. I won't occupy a small, convenient spot on your dresser. I won't blend in with your nice, tidy house and your nice, tidy life. They will carry my mark. And so,' he said, stroking a finger inside her shirt collar to tweak her bra-strap, 'will you. You'll have to get used to it.'

Her pulses boomed in her ears. He was arrogant, overbearing—and the tender touch of his hand and the smell of his bare skin so close above her was driving her crazy. I love him and I hate him, she thought. 'For as long as it takes, anyway,' she said scathingly.

Haze frowned. 'What?'

'To finish this—what did you call it?—this *unresolved tension* between us. That was what you proposed, wasn't it?' she said. 'That we should have an affair and keep on having it until it fades out naturally?'

For a heart-stopping moment she thought he was going to deny it was what he wanted. His eyes darkened in anger followed quickly by sober speculation. 'That was my proposition,' he agreed, his eyes on her mouth. 'And I stand by it. Until it fades out naturally. Get used to me, Laura-love, this could take some time.'

His kiss was an exercise in versatility. It was as if he wanted her to remember every variation of their love-making. The teasing, the tender, the possessive, the frankly raunchy. By the time he lifted his head, the marks of her fingernails were on his shoulders and she was gasping for breath. Haze inspected the change in her expression with growing smugness. 'I like the way you look when I've kissed you,' he said, letting her up at last.

She made her escape, aware that if she didn't move now she might end up spending the morning in bed with him. Lori hated herself for being tempted. Was the pull of him so strong, was she so weak that years of discipline and purpose could be discarded at a whim?

In the mirror she glimpsed herself, tousled, flushed, her mouth devoid of lipstick and sheened with moisture. She cast one look back at him. He was up on his feet, all six-foot-plus of him. A perfect specimen. No, not perfect. His shoulders were too wide—out of proportion. Glorious imperfection, though. Lori ran her tongue over her lips.

'Will you wear that look for me all day and never take it off until you shower?' Haze said slyly.

As she hurried out and banged the door she heard his laughter. She never had managed to wipe the smile off his face. But she smiled herself, all the way to the office as the rain beat against the windscreen. Never had she failed so dismally at something and enjoyed it so much.

# CHAPTER TEN

ROBERT'S condition had so improved that the hospital had agreed to him travelling. 'The company is paying for a nurse to come with us. Oh, I can't wait to get back home,' Jackie said that night as she searched the kitchen for toys and belongings that Amanda had scattered during her stay. 'I'm leaving the hire car at the airport for Haze...

'Oh, I forgot. He said to tell you that he had to fly to Hobart to see some Tasmanian wilderness expert before he vanishes into the wilds of the north-west—the expert that is, not Haze.' She giggled. 'He said he'll ring you later to tell you what time he'll be back on the mainland.'

'Oh, right,' Lori said drily, none too pleased to find out about her husband's activities from her sister-in-law. Tasmania? She did some quick reckoning of the flight times as she set out salad vegetables for a light meal. Allow, say, four hours for the interview and waiting for airline schedules, and he would probably be home by ten tonight.

Her body tingled with anticipation. She had time for a long, scented bath. And there was the new peach-colored satin nightgown she had bought in a secretive shopping trip between appointments today. Lori smiled, already forgiving him for not phoning in person. When he arrived, she would have coffee and brandy ready— and chocolates to cater for his sweet tooth. She'd pick some of Woody's iceberg roses from the garden, dim the lights...

She drifted off, thinking of Haze, hearing his voice. 'Get used to me, Laura-love, this could take some time.' It was almost a declaration of love. He wanted the marriage to be real; he'd already said that. Tonight, Lori decided. Tonight I will tell him that I love him. She bit her lip at the enormity of it. What would happen to all her plans, her goals in life? They had been drawn up not allowing for anyone else in the picture—let alone a man like Haze Callahan, who would not be confined to a tiny corner of her life.

Remembering his steely warning that morning, she smiled with a tinge of resentment and an odd sort of pride that he was the kind of man he was.

'...hear she was at your cousin's exhibition last night?'

Lori blinked, aware that she had missed several vital seconds of Jackie's conversation. 'Sorry—who?'

'Justine. Well, she will have got the message once and for all at last. I feel sorry for her, but honestly, she put Haze through a terrible time. Obsessive men give me the creeps, but an obsessive woman!' She shuddered. 'It's so pathetic.'

'Obsessive?'

Jackie bit her lip and eyed Lori uncertainly, as if she felt she had been undiplomatic. 'I probably wouldn't say this if you weren't the mature, confident type. You probably know that they had a—a thing going at one time. Only for a little over a year.'

Only a *year*. Mature and confident Lori felt a splinter of pure jealousy pierce her. An affair that had lasted over a year had to have cemented powerful feelings—feelings that would not easily be dismissed. Did Haze still see Justine? Well, of course he didn't...if he'd planned to do that, he never would have let Justine believe his marriage was the genuine thing.

She smiled dreamily as she filled a bowl with cold water and ice cubes. He would be home before ten. The sandalwood bath salts or the jasmine bubble bath? Would the jasmine be a bit too obvious—a bit Arabian Nights-ish?

Still. She frowned. 'Obsessive?' she said again.

Jackie wrinkled her nose. 'Justine couldn't accept that it was over. She moved from the coast afterwards, you know, and deliberately bought that house not far from Haze's place.'

Lori washed tomatoes under running water. Her hands were freezing. Rain streamed down the window. It was a night for hearty soups and stews, but she stuck to her health diet of salad three nights a week no matter what. Just now she was feeling chilled at the prospect. 'No. I didn't know.'

'Kept dropping in to see him, phoning at night, sending presents, certain she could rekindle the fire. Worst of all, she made her son nearly as obsessive as herself—I think she convinced Tony that if he tried hard enough he could have Haze as a father. The kid was already neurotic because his real father was such a stinker, and of course he hero-worshipped Haze. I often wonder if he got stuck on that cliff on purpose...'

Lori tossed one, then the other tomato in the ice-water. Why didn't she want to hear this? 'Surely not.'

Jackie shrugged. 'Funny how something always happened to drag Haze back into their lives and give Justine an excuse to cry on his shoulder. I kept telling him he was too soft, that he should point-blank refuse to have anything more to do with her, but he said he felt a certain responsibility and didn't want to hurt either of them if he could help it. Well, I don't need to tell you what he's like.'

Jackie pounced on a stuffed purple giraffe, lodged behind the bread crock, then sifted through the pile of toys in her arms. 'Amanda—where have you put your teddy bear, lovey?' she called as she went out.

Lori took down a colander from her overhead rack and unwrapped celery and endive. So that explained his change of mind about her lunatic proposition. She remembered now that brief look of calculation on his face when they'd been on the beach. Maybe then he had already been considering the value of a marriage of convenience as a bulwark against Justine and her son.

How did you convince an obsessive ex-lover that there was no possibility of rekindling the fire? By throwing water on the sparks, stomping on them, shovelling earth over ashes. And she—clever Lori Tate—had been so *thrilled* to find out that he'd never told Justine the marriage was a fake. So *delighted* because she'd thought it meant something special.

She sliced off the base of the bunch of celery with one executioner stroke. That wasn't why he had kept the nature of their marriage such a close secret. That wasn't why he'd arranged such a romantic wedding. He hadn't secretly languished for Lori Tate and wanted a real wedding, a real marriage—he'd wanted to make sure Justine believed it was the real thing. And if his family and friends believed it, then Justine could hardly do otherwise. 'Check that no spark remains to start another fire . . .'

And if Lori Tate herself was smitten too, all the better. She allowed herself to dwell on his early-morning charm, the warm approval in his eyes at the gallery, his gallantry in rushing to her side at the police station. Her jaw clenched. She was stupid. Gullible. Celery sticks plunked into the bowl—arrows into icy water. She should have seen it coming . . . *would* have, if she had stuck to her self-imposed rules and not allowed the charismatic Callahan to cloud her judgement.

There had been too many coincidences. He'd turned up at the island . . . swum right to the rock where she had been tamely waiting, thinking she was centre-stage but all the time only playing out a bit part in Act II of cool-hand Callahan's script. And he'd had the nerve to pretend that *she* was the siren, drawing him to her against his will! Clever. After one meeting the man had known that she liked to feel in control and he'd played on it. The knife-edge screeched on the chopping board as she scraped celery scraps into the bin.

Second coincidence. He had come uninvited to Fairlie's exhibition, where he had just *happened* to run into Justine—with his new wife conveniently beside him. And how *possessively* he'd held on to the little woman, flaunted the wife to the former mistress who had become such a nuisance with her obsession for the big, strong hunk in hiking boots. Frilly green fragments went flying as Lori tore the endive apart and tossed it in the colander.

And last night? She snipped some thyme and basil from the herbs on her window ledge, added the leaves to oil and vinegar in a jar. She shook the jar vigorously. Last night. Images flashed in her mind in quick succession, like picture cards dealt out by an expert hand. One kept repeating: Haze, lunging across the bed to pick up the phone.

Coldly she forced herself to view it in a modern sense. One night with a sexy, raunchy lover; that was all it was. A very necessary release of sexual tension for the stressed career woman. She really had to stop herself weaving romantic situations around Haze Callahan and everything he did. He was a man with a lusty appetite, and last night that had suited her. Furiously she shook the jar of dressing. Hello, goodbye, and in between fun, passion, tenderness. No strings. Hordes of women who read *Cosmopolitan* would envy her the experience.

The salad dressing was frothing.

Amanda skipped into the kitchen and threw her arms around Lori's hips. 'Goodbye, Auntie Lori. You're coming to visit us when Daddy's better, aren't you?' she said. 'I'll show you my cubby-house.'

'Lovely,' Lori said in a husky voice. She picked up Haze's niece and cuddled her. 'I'm going to miss you.'

Jackie kissed her, a little tearful as she thanked her for everything. 'Next time you and Haze can make it up north together, we want you to come to dinner,' she said. 'How *are* you going to work things—I mean, with you in Melbourne and him in Queensland?' She banished her curiosity with some embarrassment. 'Sorry, none of my business. I dare say you'll have one of those unconventional marriages... We never thought Haze would be happy with a conventional woman, so you're perfect for him. I'm so glad to have you for a sister-in-law.'

Her final hug was quick and so affectionate that Lori swallowed a lump in her throat. Now, she thought. She ought to tell Jackie right now that there was no marriage, conventional or unconventional, just a business deal and some unresolved tensions that they were in the process of resolving. But she didn't. The hire car vanished down the drive and out into the evening traffic.

Lori walked through the quiet house, conscious of being alone in a way she'd not experienced before. She ran her fingertips along the edge of Woody's hand-made bookshelves. This warm and loved old house seemed suddenly an empty space, offering only the bare survival comfort of shelter from the rain. The thought seemed a betrayal of her godmother, who had lived out her independent, fruitful life in contentment, yet, though she tried, Lori could not recover the pleasure she had always felt in this place.

Now that anger no longer gripped her, hope came sidling in. Maybe she was misinterpreting things. But the voice of the devil's advocate kept whispering that it was all too neat. All too obvious provided you took off your rose-coloured glasses. Haze might have meant some of the things he'd said in the heat of the moment, but today he hadn't even found time to phone her himself and say he'd had to fly to Tasmania.

She went to the bedroom and looked around, finding no trace of him save the book of poetry he had taken from Woody's shelves, his place marked by an envelope.

The phone rang later, but it was a stranger's voice that passed on a message from Mr Callahan to say that he had been delayed and would not now fly back to the mainland tonight. Coldly she picked up the satin nightgown, folded it into a tight little bundle and tossed it in a drawer.

She was on site the next afternoon, high in an office block being built by Tate's. Antarctic winds swept in through the skeletal framework, and Lori shivered in her padded jacket.

'Someone coming up to see Ms Tate.' The ground foreman's voice came through on the radio. Cables rippled as the gantry started its ascent and Lori hunched over the engineer's plans and wondered which of the architects was on his way and what problem was coming with him.

It wasn't a hard-hatted architect who stepped out of the gantry, but Haze. Lori gaped. 'What are you doing here?' she said coldly, even as her heart raced.

Haze narrowed his eyes at the patent lack of welcome, and looked so formidable that the engineer and off-siders shuffled away, saying they had to look at the north face. 'I don't know why,' he said sardonically, 'but I thought you'd be pleased to see me.'

Such conceit. One night with him and he thought she would be putty in his hands. Lori stoically avoided thinking of that night, or of his hands for that matter. 'Not wearing your T-shirt with the fire-extinguishing tips?' she said. 'I suppose you hardly need it any more. You should have put out every last little spark by now.'

Mystified, but angry at her tone, he set his hands on his hips. He was a big man, bundled up in a thick woollen jumper under his Navajo patterned jacket, and should have looked like the Michelin man, but didn't. 'Explain,' he bit out.

'Jackie told me about Justine,' she said. 'You could have let me in on it before you involved me in that little charade at the gallery. I'm sure being married to me was very useful in convincing her that it's all over, but I don't appreciate being manipulated just to make a point with your ex-girlfriend.'

She waited a moment but he made no reply, just stared at her, his jaw rigid. 'I see now why you lunged across the bed to grab the phone,' she went on. 'You knew poor, obsessive Justine would have to phone to see if you really *were* with me, because she wasn't quite convinced we were a devoted couple, was she? But she heard *your* voice and, of course, you announced yourself— just to make sure she was in no doubt. I suppose you planned to be in my bed that night for that very purpose!'

A muscle flickered in his jaw. 'You called me, remember?' he said, his voice harsh. 'From the police station?'

Lori had perceived this flaw in her argument much earlier, but now, as then, elected to dismiss it. 'I expect you would have just turned up at my door if I hadn't, wouldn't you? You had your plans made.'

He looked her over, eyes narrowed, and she observed his expression alter. 'You don't believe that,' he said, his voice caressing and infinitely dangerous. It had been much easier to keep track of her grievances against him last night, she thought desperately. 'You've gone on the attack suddenly...you're fighting hard to find some cast-iron reason to back off from me.' He stepped forward as he spoke, and, gallingly, she physically backed off, as if to prove his point. Haze smiled.

Lori felt the bulk of a cold steel girder behind her. Haze closed the distance between them to take advantage of her trapped position. 'I half expected this. You're not accustomed to sharing your life—you told me that. You like to be in control and suddenly you weren't—you wanted me and you told me so, and there's nothing wrong with that, Laura-love.'

'Don't patronise me,' she said, furious at that indulgent tone in his voice, scared by the weakness that made her crave his warmth and strength on any condition.

'"I need you," you said, and I came running because I never thought I would hear those words from the supercool Ms Tate, who runs all her races on her own and likes it that way.' He moved in close, bent and lightly touched his lips to her temple.

The casual contact rocked her. Lori despaired at the weapons he had at his disposal. Those who loved were bound to be at the mercy of the loved one who only wanted.

'Mmm. The sweetest words I ever heard,' he said, and she saw the glitter of triumph in his eyes.

'Well, you'd hardly expect me to ring Mark or The Uncles to come and pick me up at the police station, would you?' she said tartly. 'I would never hear the end of it.'

His eyes narrowed, but the moment of doubt passed. 'You're saying I was a convenient choice?' He shook his head, smiled. 'No, Laura-love, that won't wash. You wanted *me*—I heard it in your voice, saw it in your face. If you hadn't been involved in that little fracas, you would have found some other excuse to phone me. Admit it.'

Lori flushed. 'You're so arrogant.'

He laughed softly. 'When that policeman said "your wife" that really shook me, and I knew then—' He took off her hard-hat, curved the palm of his hand over her hair, smoothing the strands that had lifted with the hat. His fingertips traced her brow and down the side of her face to her mouth. Lori's lips parted. If she remained silent now she was lost. 'Speak now, or else hereafter for ever hold your peace...'

'What did you know?' she said scornfully. 'I think I should tell you, Haze, that you shouldn't make too much of the fact that I used your name that night.'

He smiled. 'Mrs Callahan... I admit I got a buzz out of it. More than a buzz. Lori Tate acknowledging me as her husband in public. It was music to my ears, Lauralove. I knew it was only a matter of time after that.'

He was so smugly sure of her and she was so uncertain of him. The one-sidedness of it hurt, struck at her pride. In years of negotiation as a woman in a man's world, she'd never felt at such a disadvantage.

'It suited me to be Mrs Callahan at the time,' she told him. 'I recognised a Press reporter there. He didn't notice me in my bedraggled state, but if he'd caught one whiff of the Tate name—well,' she said with a small shrug of one shoulder, 'I didn't fancy being featured in the newspapers as a participant in a street fracas. It wouldn't enhance my reputation with the board—especially right now when I'm running for Carson's position as head of Colussus.'

She hoped he would not remember how little she had cared for her reputation at the gallery, when she had been busy insulting Uncle Clark and sundry others.

Haze was very still, his arms either side of her, his hands on the steel girder. She felt his breath, warm on her mouth, and he stayed there close enough to kiss for the count of twenty. He had missed a few whiskers again when he'd shaved, she noticed. Perhaps he'd been in a hurry this morning. She felt a pang deep inside her. In a hurry to see her? Doubt assailed her.

Her eyes flickered to his, saw them widened in hurt surprise, and she almost took back the words. But once said, words couldn't be taken back, and Haze was drawing away from her, his warmth receding until there was a space between him and her and only the chill of steel behind.

His smile was self-deprecating. 'You'll probably get a laugh out of this, Ms Tate, but I never thought of that.' He took a few paces around the scaffolding. 'I was too wound up by hearing you tell me you needed me to remember that you always have a sound, practical reason for everything you do.' Still holding her helmet, he paused and looked out at the city and the sky through the open space framed in scaffolding and girders.

He turned again to her. 'Incredible, isn't it, that a grown man could be such a bloody, credulous fool?' He snorted. 'It was never going to work with us anyway, except for the sex. The sex,' he said deliberately, 'was great. You're one hell of a woman when you forget to be a man.'

Lori's head went back. 'Keep your voice down.'

His eyes glittered. He came close to her and she felt his anger jab at her as he lowered his voice. 'Afraid your colleagues might find out what a wanton you can be? That the ice-cool director can moan and writhe and leave nail-marks on my skin? That Ms Lorelei Tate can beg for her pleasure... "Please Haze. Please...hurry..."'

Her face suffused with colour, she raised a hand to strike him. Whether she would have or not she didn't know, but Haze grabbed her wrist. He closed his eyes briefly, his thumb stroking the heel of her hand with a tenderness that tapped some inner reservoir of hope. Her pulse boomed in her ears. Words spoke themselves in her brain, but the signal system to her tongue seemed frozen. If Haze said something now to account for that bitter note in his voice, that air of desolation about him— *something* ...

'My apologies. I'm a bad loser,' he said.

Her pulse-rate steadied to a dull march-beat. So that was all it was. She should have recognised the signs. After all, she was familiar enough with the male love of chal-

lenge and dislike of losing. Had he wanted her to fall so
badly for him that she would settle for whatever was
convenient for him? All those masterful warnings about
how *he* would not be a tame presence in her life probably
summed up just what he wanted *her* to be. *She* was to
be the tame lover, content to be invited in now and then
when he was not out trampling the wilderness under his
big feet. *She* was to occupy a small, convenient spot in
*his* life.

He was just an arm's length from her, planted solidly
on the boards, but moving further away with every
second that passed in silence from her. Maybe, she
thought wildly, it wouldn't be so bad. He would be
around sometimes, away sometimes. He didn't want
strong ties. Surely that fitted perfectly with the demands
of her life? And if he was arrogant and wanted to feel
that he was in control all the time...so what? She was
used to dealing with men who wanted to run everything
and everyone.

Her brief attempt at self-deception died. There was
no way she could give herself over to a relationship so
unequal. She loved him and it was wishful thinking to
suppose that anything less than love from him would do.
Lori suppressed a hysterical laugh. And Haze thought
*he* was the loser. At least she could salvage that bit of
balm for her pride.

The sound of voices below grew louder. The gantry
cables slid past outside the sky-space framed in
scaffolding.

'Here come your colleagues.' Haze turned the hard-
hat in his hands, then reached out and put it on her
head. 'Not that you need it,' he said sardonically.
'Goodbye. I'll see my solicitor and get the divorce papers
rolling.'

The gantry appeared; the men got out. There was some
small-talk and Haze shook hands with them before he
got into the gantry. By the time it began its slow descent,

the engineer had unrolled the blueprints for Lori's benefit. She held the plans and looked past them at Haze, outlined against the sky and slipping away. He lifted his head at the last moment, and she caught one final flash of those dark eyes then he was gone.

'As you can see, we're well ahead on schedule with the reinforcement . . .' the engineer was saying, pointing to the plans Lori held in her outstretched arms. She looked blankly at the lines and symbols and forced herself to make some sensible response.

For another twenty minutes she made sensible responses, and all the time she remained sharply aware of the movement of the cables and the clanking that accompanied the journey of the gantry down the outside of the building. Her eyes followed the engineer's finger as it roamed over the plans while her mind remarked that the cables had stopped moving, signalling that Haze had reached the ground.

And long after her mind had pictured him striding away she made more sensible comments while she stood inside a shell of a building and a cold wind carrying rain blew through its unprotected spaces.

# CHAPTER ELEVEN

'LORI, the charity committee and the Lord Mayor will be arriving in about twenty minutes,' her secretary said as she laid a sheaf of papers on the desk. 'All the ropes are in place on the roof and the abseilers are in the car park, harnessing up. The Press want some shots of you wishing them luck.'

Lori sighed, eased away from her document-piled desk and looked down with resignation at a run in her tights. 'Thanks, Sandra. Have you got me a list of names of the committee?'

Sandra riffled through a file and withdrew a sheet. 'Here. I've got some spares, if you're out of them,' she said, indicating the laddered tights with a dip of her head.

'I've got some, thanks.' Taking a spare pair from her bottom drawer, Lori went to her sitting room and studied the sheet of paper while she rolled off the old and rolled on the new.

At her desk again, Lori gazed past her jungle of palms, through the glass wall at the city sprawl of Brisbane. This was the view she had wanted for years. She was sitting in the chair she had hankered for, in the office with her name and 'Chief Executive, Colussus' inscribed on a copper panel on the door, the way she had always imagined it. Ironic that once she had stopped wanting it so much it had dropped in her lap.

The February sky was a clear, cloudless blue—a rare thing for Melbourne, but commonplace here in the subtropics. As commonplace as the tropical storms that swept in with sudden fury and vanished, leaving creamy frangipani blossoms and cerise bougainvillaea flowers scattered and the hot street surfaces steaming.

At one time Lori had thought that she wouldn't like to leave Melbourne and Woody's house, the closest thing to a home she'd had since she was nine. But when two months had passed after that August day in an unfinished building, she'd found she was less attached to Woody's house than she'd thought. And when she had got here, where she'd always wanted to be, it, too, had failed to ground her.

It was as if she were in some kind of limbo, fully functioning in many ways, but with no ties to any place—not belonging to where she'd been or to where she'd come. So where was home?

'Lori, the Mayor's car is just turning into the car park—early I'm afraid,' Sandra said through the intercom.

'I'm on my way.' Lori brushed her hair, flicked some lint off her suit jacket with a brush, rearranged the soft tie neckline of her blouse and reapplied lipstick. She was busy, and this charity event was time-consuming, but Colussus had a track record for supporting community groups and it was valuable in terms of public relations.

Whether the publicity stunt of a team of intrepid climbers abseiling down the side of the Colussus building would translate into a more profitable doorknock appeal for muscular dystrophy was dubious. But she had given her permission for the Colussus building to be used, so inevitably had to be part of yet another ritual of handshaking and small talk.

She took the elevator down with Sandra and found crowds of staff moving into the car park. There would be little work done in Colussus this morning, she thought wryly, hoping that at least the security people would stay on the job while everyone was downstairs gawking at the climbers.

Lori assumed a smile as she welcomed the mayoral party and the fund-raising committee, two of whom were in wheelchairs. Tiny red lights blinked on television cameras as they turned in their direction from the group of jumpsuited, helmeted climbers whose harnesses jingled with dangling karabiners. Photographers moved in close as the two groups converged for the jolly spontaneous hand-shaking preliminaries.

'Good luck,' Lori said, smiling at one climber after another, reading the names stitched onto their suits. 'Good luck, Jim. Good luck, Lynette. Philip. Jason. Good luck—' she said to the second-last climber, glancing at his name, registering the shape and sound of it in the same moment as she looked into his eyes. Darkest blue eyes. Dark brows and lashes. Tanned skin and a mouth to dream about. A mouth she *had* dreamed about '—Haze,' she finished.

'Thank you, ma'am.'

The voice was the same. Strange how the memory could not store up the actual sound of a voice but as soon as you heard it you knew if it was the one. 'Haze,' she said again, looking him over, checking out the details. He looked marvellous, wide-shouldered and athletic in the baggy jumpsuit. But then, a man who could score nine out of ten in a wetsuit would.

She checked him out again for injury, an occupational hazard for him. Sometimes she had woken at night, dreaming of him disappearing under white water, hurtling into space from a precipice. But he was whole and bore no visible scars save the lightning flash of the scar on his left thumb. She never had asked him how he'd done that.

'Haze,' she said yet again, reading it off his suit.

'If you don't stop saying my name, people will talk. At least one of those Press people over there knows we're married. Why haven't you signed the divorce papers yet, by the way? It's not like the efficient CE of Colussus to procrastinate.'

She looked around at the Press people, suddenly jolted out of her daze by his amused, mocking tone. 'You could have warned me,' she said. 'Or is this your idea of a tasteless joke—like an orchid-pink limousine with a stupid bride-doll on the front?'

'I was rather hoping you'd be at your desk when I made my descent. I would have waved to you as I passed by,' he said, doing some checking out of his own. 'You've softened your image.' He flicked a finger at the soft bow of aqua georgette at her neck. His hand rose, but stopped short of actually touching her hair. 'I love your hair loose like that.'

He stopped abruptly and looked down as he pulled on leather gauntlets, and Lori got the impression that he hadn't meant to say that the way he had—without the irony that had tinged everything else so far. 'I love your hair...' Anything else? she wondered.

'Jackie's in the Mater Hospital in Brisbane,' he told her abruptly. 'Some minor complications with her pregnancy. She said if I saw you to tell you to visit—with or without flowers. Always the optimist, Jackie.'

'Complications? What kind of—?'

But the last climber pushed forward, grinning and holding out his hand. When Lori automatically took it, he said, 'Wow! Cold hands.'

Cold hands. 'Then, warm them, Laura-love...' Lori's eyes met Haze's mocking blue ones, and the closest Colussus staff were privileged to witness a rare occurrence as their chief executive blushed crimson.

'Warm heart,' Haze said drily.

The abseilers marched in formation, turning to wave to the onlookers at the doors like astronauts about to enter a spacecraft. Lori looked up at the Colussus building. As skyscrapers went it was an infant, but suddenly the glassy walls seemed to soar for ever. Straight down. She gulped, seeing Haze's flying body silhouetted against an azure sky.

For a moment she remained rooted to the ground, properly aware of the place and the occasion. Then, without conscious decision, she ran forward as the climbers went through the building doors. Haze turned back at the sound of her heels on marble steps and watched in astonishment as she ran to him.

And now that she was here, she couldn't think. Her mouth opened and shut as she stared into his face. Her hands made several awkward flights in the air and settled on his arms.

'Be careful,' she said lamely. 'Please be careful.'

His eyes narrowed. 'Worried you might have put a hex on me? Worried you might have wished me good luck but brought me bad?' His arm went around her waist. 'Let's dispel that myth once and for all, shall we?' His gauntleted hands spread on her back and crushed her to him, and she felt the hard edge of his helmet as he kissed her.

There was nothing soft and sweet about this kiss. It was intense and passionate, opening immediately to a desperate kind of intimacy. Lori pressed closer, feeling the cold bite of metal harness buckles, not caring for anything but the taste of him, the feel of him in her arms and the sense of an end to some nameless longing. There was the tinkling sound of bells.

When they separated at last, Haze was as out of breath as she. He held her at arm's length, his lips apart and sheened with moisture, his nostrils flaring with each breath.

'Rumour has it that your marriage is on the rocks,' said a woman's voice behind them. She held out a small microphone to catch any reply.

Haze drew a gloved hand across his mouth and grinned. 'You be the judge. We like to keep everyone guessing.'

Then he spun around and followed the others inside to the elevator, his harness jingling.

The stunt was a success and over in mere minutes. Heart in mouth, Lori stared up at the glittering Colussus building, shading her eyes with one hand. Six ropes snaked over the side and shortly afterwards six suited figures appeared. Lori watched only one. Haze loped face-first down the vertical surface, his mouth open in the wordless yell of challenge or bravado that each climber made. She closed her eyes briefly as he reached the ground, unclenched her fists. Of course, the man did this kind of thing all the time. It was stupid, *stupid* to worry about him.

But as the event wound down and she prepared to take the mayoral party inside for tea and biscuits in the VIP reception room, Lori's eyes kept straying to the figure of the big man removing his harness. He took off his helmet and she saw that his hair was longer. Not nearly long enough to wrap around her fingers, but not that short nap he'd sported before either.

If only she didn't have all these visitors, she would go to him...and say what? Haze met her eyes across the car park as he put his harness and helmet in the back of his four-wheel-drive. He sketched a mocking little salute, then, as another climber got into the passenger seat, he got in and drove off.

As the vehicle turned from the Colussus car park it was momentarily out of the sun's glare. On its side, in ghostly letters, Lori saw the scrawled words 'Just Married'. But as soon as the sunlight hit the paintwork again, the imprint vanished.

'Be careful.' It was something women always said. His mother, his sister. 'Be careful'—as if somehow he might forget to be careful when he was dangling on a rope, or crossing some God-forsaken desert. His mother told him he shouldn't interpret such feeble warnings literally, that it was an expression of caring, a way of saying 'It would hurt me if anything bad happened to you'.

Haze sat in the pub with the other climbers, pondering the possible interpretations of Lorelei Tate. Would it hurt her if he was harmed? Or had that pallor and that gut-wrenching look of anxiety in those beautiful grey eyes simply been from fear that she might again be a jinx. The Hex.

Absently, he smiled. The dreaded X-words. Funny that such a hard-headed woman was actually superstitious. Oh, she disguised it in nonchalant wit, but he'd begun to read the signposts to all the things she kept suppressed. At least, he'd thought he had.

Wryly he raised his glass and made some response to Lynette, who kept trying to drag his attention back to the group. Attractive girl, Lynette, he thought, hormones momentarily sparking as he recognised Lyn's ploy for attention as something more personal. But before he'd finished a reassessment of her lush brunette good looks, his mind had drifted off.

He could have sworn Lori was crazy about him. But he could never quite get it out of his mind that she was used to having what she wanted when she wanted it...and it was plain that for the Tates that extended to people too. His hand tightened on the glass. Pure ego, of course, but he couldn't stand the thought that he might have been some toy-boy novelty in her life. Lori Tate could be so cool, so detached. And he had been acting like a gormless adolescent, wearing his heart on his sleeve, giving her all the advantages.

Good grief, Callahan. You must have been mad, thinking she would call herself Mrs Callahan for sentimental reasons. Those grey eyes had looked right through him when he'd been halfwit enough to admit that he'd gone gaga when the policeman had said 'your wife'. A cold August wind and Lori Tate's eyes...they'd had much the same effect that day on the scaffolding.

On the other hand... He frowned, picturing her at nine years old, doggedly searching an entire hospital for her missing mother. Ms Tate, the director, who blithely installed a child at the boardroom table with paper and coloured pencils. The ambitious career woman almost paranoid about her professional image, who wore a necklace made of paperclips and bits of flowered plastic with her pin-striped suit because she knew how deeply a child felt a broken promise.

Lori in his arms, passionate and generous and honest. Lori running towards him today—*running*. He was struck anew by the enormity of it. In front of all those people she had abandoned that cool dignity that she valued so much. 'Be careful...' And the way she'd looked at him... Haze stood up abruptly. What was he doing here? What was he doing even contemplating driving away from her?

He stood up, made his excuses. It was a short journey back through the Spring Hill terraces to the Colussus building. All the way Haze totted up the points in his favour: she'd kissed him back with a kind of desperation today, and hadn't given a thought to the Press cameras rolling; she hadn't signed the divorce papers; supercool Ms Tate had been flustered to see him again, tripped over her words like a stuttering schoolgirl.

He laughed softly, getting a delayed sense of the euphoria that usually followed the adrenaline rush of a fast descent. And she'd blushed. When was the last time Lori Tate had blushed in public? He turned into the Colussus car park with a triumphant flourish.

The official cars were gone. He parked and got out of the truck just as Lori emerged from the building. Smiling, he folded his arms and leaned back against the cabin, crossed one foot over the other. There were several suits with her, carrying clipboards and hard-hats, but he didn't mind waiting for that moment when she would walk towards him.

But Lori didn't do that. She looked the long distance across the car park straight at him for several seconds then gave a little shake of her head and turned to get into a silver Fairlane. The others piled in and, as the car drove away, Haze saw Lori put on sunglasses, open her attaché case and take some documents from it. Her expression was serious and her attention fully on the suit next to her. She didn't look out of the window again.

Haze looked up at the Colussus building. He felt as if he'd just leapt off the top of it without a rope. Did she think he was going to tamely stand here until she was ready? Was that scarcely discernible movement of her head meant to convey that it was inconvenient to see him right now? He got in the truck, slammed the door.

The divorce papers were probably already signed but stuck in a pile of paperwork on her lawyer's desk. That blush had probably been a response to a hot, humid February day. As for being flustered...the well-organised Ms Tate had probably just been irritated at being caught unprepared. He cursed softly under his breath as he caught a red light.

He would never understand why she'd run to him like that today, but did it matter? The fact was that Lori had been planning all her life to be where she was today. A man in her life would get in the way. Viciously he swung the truck northwards. If she wanted him, she could damned well run to him. But she wouldn't, so that was that. He took the Bruce Highway exit. Exit. Another bloody awful X-word.

The florist had put some stems of tuberose in the mixed bouquet that Lori carried. Half her memories must be tied up in her sense of smell, she thought. The perfume of the flowers tormented her, conjuring up rainforest greens and sunlight and lacy shadows at odds with the polished corridor and the unmistakable blend of hospital smells that brought back other, darker times. Her hand clenched around the flower stems, crushing the tissue wrapping.

She never went inside a hospital if she had a choice. But she'd seen Haze again and, now that he'd vanished, she foolishly wanted some contact with him, even if it was only talking to his sister. Besides, it had moved her, that warm message from Jackie whom she hadn't seen for six months. She had tried to cut her ties with Haze's family, but had had a note each from Meg and Jackie and several multi-coloured drawings in the post from Amanda. The Callahans just never gave up on a person, Lori thought, caught between exasperation and pleasure. At least, the Callahan women didn't.

Lori shifted the blue-wrapped parcel under her arm and tensed herself for a room full of Callahans—or at least a room full of one particular Callahan. Some adolescent part of her had hoped Haze would be here. But there was only a freckled red-haired man by Jackie's bed.

'Robert Duncan,' he introduced himself as he vigorously shook her hand. 'Thanks a heap for all you did when I was in hospital in Melbourne. Amanda talks about you all the time.'

Jackie took the flowers and hugged Lori, subjecting her to a keen appraisal before she directed her attention to Master Christopher Duncan, asleep in a cradle beside the bed. Lori looked at the sleeping black-haired mite. New life was amazing. She looked in awe at Jackie.

'Two weeks early; he took us all by surprise. I was about to be released from hospital when I went into labour. Mum's on her way to Brisbane with Amanda, but they still don't know Daniel has arrived. And we haven't been able to tell Haze.' Some of her joy dissipated.

'I wish I could get word to him—I know he's worried about my blood pressure. He's on an exercise for a week—an advanced class. They've already switched off

all the radios and phones, and once they leave the house
area and disperse in all those acres of rainforest, no one
will find them for days with the news...'

Robert frowned and started to say something, but
Jackie grabbed his hand in both of hers and gazed up
at him with meaningful eyes. 'Oh—say hello to my room-
mate, Bronwyn,' she said to Lori, who frowned at what
seemed a deliberate distraction, but dutifully turned to
greet the woman in the other bed. 'She was early too.'

'This was my third,' said Bronwyn serenely. 'They've
all been early.'

There was an air of feminine achievement in the room.
The maternity ward had gone some way to curing her
aversion to hospitals, Lori decided. Jackie's triumphant
mood slipped, though, as she worried aloud about
getting the word from Brisbane to Haze.

'What about Tom?' Lori ventured. 'He could drive
out—'

'Oh, Tom's away,' Jackie said, grabbing her husband's hand again. 'I suppose there must be someone
reliable, but I just can't think—' Jackie turned pleading
eyes on her. 'Lori—would *you* go? I know it might be
embarrassing for you, but it wouldn't take long and I
just can't relax until I know someone is on the way to
tell him...' She put her hands to her breasts, looking at
her newborn son, as if the worry might affect her milk.

Fly north to see Haze before he vanished into his rainforest? It was the last thing she wanted to do. She was
a busy person. There was paperwork to do tonight and
an early appointment tomorrow, and already she was
behind schedule for today just making this visit this
morning. It was ridiculous—the whim of a woman whose
hormones were on the rampage.

Her own hormones seemed to be suddenly very
unstable.

'All right,' she said. 'I'll go.'

Jackie beamed. 'You'll find him and tell him? Christopher Robert, three and a half kilos, born at eleven-twenty last night. Promise?'

Fly north to see Haze before he vanished into his rain-forest? It was the thing she wanted to do more than anything. There was more than one thing she had to tell Haze Callahan. 'I promise,' she said, and drew her mobile phone from her bag, punched out her travel agent's number.

At home she packed an overnight bag, and at the last moment she put in the book of poetry, marked at his place. On the flight, she thought, she would open it and see what it was that Haze had been reading. But though she held the book on her lap, she was too distracted by her thoughts and didn't open it.

She arrived on the Queensland coast just after noon, hired a car from the same company and took the same road past the office of Callahan's Survival School, where a flicker of movement made her smile. So Tom was away, was he? Past the patch of road where Justine had cut in front of the four-wheel-drive. There was a 'For Sale' sign outside the pillared gateway with the carved lions.

Lori eased off the accelerator when she turned onto the unsealed road that led to Haze's property. The last time she'd been here was in May, in a car with 'Just Married' written on it in shaving cream. February was monsoon season up here, and, though the road surface was dry and dusty now, there were boggy patches of mud to watch out for.

It was the vehicle going the other way that caused the trouble. The dust from its passing swirled like fog across the windscreen and Lori hit a pothole and ran off the dry surface into mud. The wheels spun, sinking deeper into the mire. She got out and stared at it in dismay. She should have hired a four-wheel-drive. Lori grimaced. Haze would say 'I told you so'.

'Oh, I don't believe it.' The sound of the other car had long faded into silence. She could phone for assistance or for another car, but how long would that take?

An urgency gripped her. She had the kind of superstitious feeling that she'd had as a child...

Something bad might happen if she failed to step on *every* dark brown brick on the driveway, if she didn't get up the stairs without making them creak, if she didn't get to the next corner on the count of five. If she didn't get to Haze before he vanished into the rainforest for a week, he might vanish for ever.

This time she was at least dressed for the terrain, in linen shorts, a singlet and a jacket. Thoughtfully she looked down at her shoes. Not ideal, but soft leather lace-ups with sturdy soles. It would be twelve miles, maybe more. About the length of a half-marathon. But she'd run further for no reason at all, run just to clock up times with nothing substantial at the end of it. So Lori ran.

It was one-thirty when she left the car and nearly four when she reached the gateway marked 'Callahan'. Slow for someone who had run a half-marathon in her PB of one hour forty-six minutes. But the weather was hot, there were blisters on her feet and she had rationed her intake of fluids to make a half-finished carton of fruit juice bought at the airport last the distance.

She limped along the rutted drive, her crisp linen jacket tied around her waist and drooping behind her, her hair stuck to her scalp with perspiration. The sight of his house roused her to a jog again. There was no sign of activity there, but beyond it she made out the movement of figures on the track that wound off through eucalyptus and scrub into the wild acres of his land.

'Haze!' she yelled. But she hadn't breath enough to propel her voice so far. Doggedly she went on. If she kept her pace faster than theirs, she had to catch them

soon. The track straightened out and she saw the group
of walkers ahead, laden with backpacks. As she drew
closer the sound of her approach reached them and they
turned. Lori shook sweat from her eyes, fixed on one
figure in khaki shorts and shirt and boots.

Even at this distance it was perfectly clear that his
shoulders were out of proportion to the rest of him. Lori
found a last turn of speed and lengthened her stride. So
much easier to find that bit extra when there was something substantial at the end of it all. There were no
guarantees, no certainties... she still didn't know if he
really loved her.

The doubt made her falter until she saw Haze take off
his hat and skim it into the bushes. He shrugged out of
the backpack and discarded it. Then he was striding towards her. Galloping. Oh, yes. Much more satisfying
when there was a reason for it all. Someone to run to,
to run *for*. The only thing she could guarantee was her
own feeling for Haze, but there were times when you
had to take risks.

Lori would have laughed if she'd had the breath for
it. Her legs pumped through the last few steps then she
was blessedly lifted off her blistering feet, enclosed in
strong arms and treated to the music of her name being
said again and again in that voice that she never could
reproduce in her memory but which was always there.

She wrapped her arms around his neck and kissed him
awkwardly, not bothering with exact locations because
any part of Haze was worth kissing. Any little bit of him
that chanced by her mouth, she kissed. 'Where the hell
have you come from?' he demanded between kisses.
'You're coated in dust... delicious.'

'The road. Left hire car about twelve miles back.' She
waved a hand in the general direction of her stranded
vehicle. 'Ran. Got to tell you something. Promised.'

Haze knelt, cradled her, his eyes travelling over the
dirt and cuts on her legs, the bloodstains on the heels

of her tattered shoes. And when she caught enough air, Lori said, 'Christopher Robert Duncan. Three and a half kilos. Born eleven-twenty last night. Mother and baby both well.'

Haze was remarkably unmoved. 'You ran all that way to tell me that?'

She nodded, feeling light-headed. 'Something else . . . have to tell you—'

'You *ran*—on that lousy road, in those bloody ridiculous shoes,' he said in a low, savage voice, 'in this heat, with the humidity at eighty per cent? What's the matter with you, woman?'

'Had to tell you—'

'Your feet are lacerated; you're dehydrated. Don't you know the first thing about survival?' He bellowed to one of the group now gathered around to give him a water bottle.

'Had some juice,' Lori croaked, waggling the flattened juice carton at him. A dribble of mango and orange juice ran out onto her face and she licked at it and giggled.

'Bloody hell!' he muttered. 'You're delirious.'

'Had to tell you before you vanished into the rainforest for ever . . .'

'There's hardly any traffic along that road. You could have collapsed and lain there for days before anyone saw you! Drink this. Just a mouthful.'

She took a draft of water and lay back in his arms. There was not a part of her that was not hurting, but she'd never felt more alive, never felt the effort more worthwhile. 'I had to come now—right *now*. Tell you—'

'What?' he roared. 'Bloody nonsense. I already know about Jackie's baby. I've known since eleven this morning, and it was Jackie who told me!'

Lori wrinkled her nose. 'She's matchmaking. Made me promise to come and tell you because you were in-

communicado. Played on my finer feelings. That's a
Callahan trick. Couldn't have a brand-new mother so
keyed up about her anxious brother that her milk didn't
come in.'

A smile twitched at the corners of his mouth, but it
was banished by a scowl. 'I'll have a piece of her for
this. You could have killed yourself. I suppose you hired
a sedan? I *told* you that road was hell on standard
drives—'

She grinned. 'Knew you'd say "I told you so". I love
you.'

'What happened? I suppose you rammed into one of
those potholes and—' He stopped at last. Haze, the
model listener, who had almost missed the most important thing she'd ever said to him. 'What?' he asked
in a ragged voice. There was a fetching colour high on
his cheekbones, an appealing susceptibility in his widened
dark blue eyes.

Lori touched his face with trembling fingers. 'I didn't
realise it, but when I promised Jackie I'd come I was
already on my way to you. Have been for ages.' She gave
a croak of laughter that hurt her dry throat.

There was a glitter in his dark blue eyes. 'You've been
damned slow, then,' he growled.

'Mmm. But today I think I've done my personal best.'

Haze pulled her to her feet and picked her up. 'Change
of plan,' he said to the grinning members of his group.
'Back to the house.'

'You're going to carry me all that way?' Lori said. 'I
have it on good authority that I'm not exactly
thistledown.'

He grunted, and flexed his muscles to shift his hold
on her. 'I think I can manage to stagger home without
dropping you.'

Lori plucked at the collar of his shirt. 'I don't know—
that is—well—I don't know just how you feel—' She
rushed on at his startled expression. 'But it doesn't

matter. I suppose that's what I came to say. I love you and I think you have a soft spot for me, so—'

Abruptly he stopped, and stood her to her feet. '"A soft spot"!' he repeated. 'But you *know* how I feel about you, Laura-love. I've been going around like some gormless teenager with my heart on my sleeve...following you up unfinished buildings, abseiling down your windows, but trying to salvage a bit of pride here and there when I could.'

'I know how you felt about Justine,' she said, raising her chin. 'I know whenever you're with her you look—caring. I know how you feel about your family—and *my* family. But as far as I know you still think of me as a—a challenge, a compatible physical partner—and if that's it, well, I'd rather you just said so, because—'

A large dusty hand covered her mouth. He glared at her. '"A compatible physical partner"? What do you think I am? Some kind of womaniser out for a spot of slap and tickle? I love you—got that? I—love—you.'

Lori gave a brilliant smile and slipped her arms around him.

'That's all right, then.'

'Fell for you straight away,' he admitted ruefully. 'No, not straight away. But I was pretty far gone by the time you were devouring my toast on the veranda and telling me how you'd planned your life without a man in it.'

'Yes, I did. And I could live it that way, if I wanted to. But I don't want to. I want to live it with you.'

Haze swung her into his arms again and moved off vigorously towards the house. 'Well, you know what I think, Lori Callahan. You're a woman who always gets what she wants.'

Morning light lay on the veranda in golden swathes laced with shadows of fern. Down in the rainforest bell-birds called. Lori stretched and leaned over the railing, took a deep breath of air that smelled of eucalyptus and grevillea blossom. She had showered and Haze had bandaged her feet; she remembered that much. After that she must have slept.

She had woken alone, and there had been no sound save the summery buzz of insects and birdsong, so perhaps Haze had gone again, on the expedition she'd interrupted yesterday. Her bag had been by the bed when she'd woken and the hire car, its back wheels black with dried mud, was parked out front.

Vaguely disappointed, she had wandered through his lovely house looking for a note he might have left. Something simple, like 'I'll be back next week' or 'See you in Melbourne on such and such a date'. She had found none, but, beguiled by the peace and plagued by her throbbing feet, she'd sat down on the veranda and opened the book of poetry that Haze had taken from Woody's shelves six months ago.

There was nothing remarkable on the pages marked by the envelope, she saw now. She had imagined him reading this book in a blue mood of unrequited love, and had half expected the poems marked to be sonnets of love lost. Laughing at her romanticism, she closed the book. She slapped the unsealed envelope a few times, read the name of the gas company on it and then idly opened it.

It was not a gas bill. She had looked for a note from Haze this morning and now she had found one from Woody. She read the familiar writing, her eyes watering.

My dearest Lori,

I hope you will forgive me when you discover the conditions of my will. I always thought my life was a model of achievement and independence, and in its way so it was. But, Lori, I wish I could have shared it with someone, and I don't know that I made that clear to you. My dearest girl, I fear that I may have led you to value independence over all else, and I want you to know that it can be very lonely at times. I love my house and garden, but I love you more. I don't particularly care what happens to my things, but I care about you. So I hope my crazy condition will make you think...

She laughed, shedding tears at the same time. 'I already came to the same conclusion, Woody,' she said aloud, folding the letter and sliding it back between the pages of poetry. Fate that Haze had picked that book of the hundreds from Woody's shelves. She lay back and absorbed the peace.

When she opened her eyes again, he was there. Lori smiled.

'You haven't vanished into the rainforest,' she said.

'I figured if Tate's could manage without you, then my students could manage without me.' He put some salve and a packet of adhesive strips on the table and knelt beside her, began unwinding the bandages on her feet.

'I think I fell for you here, too,' she said, watching his dark head as he bent to his task. 'I was imagining your hair loose and me running my hands through it.'

'Tch, tch.' He shot her a loaded look. 'Lustful thoughts, Laura-love. I had more than a few myself.' He wound off the last length of bandage and discarded it. 'You were right, of course. I did follow you to the island. I managed to get your destination from my pal at the boat charter. He just assumed you were staying at the resort because that's where he took you. It never occurred to me that you would wade across a coral reef to stay in a tent on the other island.'

'Were you looking for me at the resort?'

'For hours,' he said. 'After I got no joy from the booking office, I roamed about describing you to people. A real waste of time, because in the meantime you'd turned into the Queen of the Jungle and looked nothing like Lorelei Tate. But someone did say they'd seen a woman wandering around alone on a beach over on the other island and that rang a bell. I'd swum practically around the whole island before I found you, half-naked.'

He grinned. 'For a moment when I surfaced I thought you were an illusion—you were too much like my fantasy of you to be true.'

She stretched like a cat in the sun, lacing her fingers behind her head so that she could watch him. As he dabbed cream on the broken blisters his shoulders were hunched forward in that sheltering way that moved her. His big hands were spread for balance, making such delicate small movements, and his tongue just showed in the corner of his mouth. What a lovely man.

'I was always seeing visions of you,' she told him. 'Once I thought I saw you in the boardroom, leaning back against the wall with your arms crossed and one ankle over the other, the way you do.'

'The boardroom?' he said cynically.

'And under the liquidamber tree in Woody's garden,' she said. 'In my bathroom—'

He leered. 'Was I starkers?'

'And once I even saw you in the Colussus car park, leaning on a car... But that was just after I'd seen you again, so I suppose it was wishful thinking.'

Haze sat back on his haunches. 'I was there. I'd come back to sweep you off your feet, but you looked right through me and went off with those suits, and I thought—'

She gaped. 'You thought I'd do that? Since when have I *ever* been able to ignore you? And don't think I didn't try. I did,' she confessed. 'That's why I had to propose to you in the end, of course. I couldn't ignore you and I couldn't resist you, so obviously the only thing I could do to save my pride was to ask you to marry me for business. I didn't really expect you to agree.'

He frowned. 'Why did you have to save your pride?'

'You were on the phone to Justine when I came out of the ladies' room at the resort that night—the phone message note was on the table—so I thought you and she really must be a couple, and that you were about to cheat on her with me as a passing fancy.'

'So you ran back to your tent.' Haze was looking very pleased indeed. Very self-assured. 'About Justine...' He drew in a deep breath. 'Look—as far as I was concerned it was over long ago, but I was fond of Justine and couldn't bring myself to be—cruel when she wouldn't let go. I hoped it would just kind of fade away for her, as it had for me.'

He was choosing his words with care, she realised, this man who could not simply shed a woman like an old coat when the affair was over. It was Justine who had been chasing him, who had done all the kissing that day on the road. Haze could have said that all the intent had been on Justine's side, but instead he had protected her dignity. 'You might have got the wrong impression,' he had said. Lori felt a warmth at his sensitivity, and a deep sorrow for Justine having had such a marvellous man and lost him.

'You said that about us,' she reminded him. 'That we should have an affair and keep on having it until it faded out naturally.'

'And I stand by it,' he said again, applying an adhesive strip to cover her heel. 'I give it no more than sixty years.'

'Nothing lasts,' Lori said, mock-wistful.

'If we weren't already married, I'd propose to you.'

'Well, you're already on your knees, so why don't you?'

'I've been metaphorically on my knees since I met you.'

She snorted. 'Not so I've noticed.'

He got up and sat on the side of the lounger. Lori moved over to make space for him.

'If I proposed to you now,' he said, tracing her hairline with one finger, 'a straight marriage proposal—not one of your architecturally symmetrical deals but a "Will you marry me?" with all the clutter and confusion and messiness that comes from sharing your life with someone—would you say yes?'

He was smiling, but there was some stray note in his voice that told her this was not quite light-hearted banter. She sat up and slid her hands around his neck and coaxed him down with her. 'For better for worse, for richer for poorer... Oh, yes, my love. Now, lie back and think of the Bank of England.'

He stretched out but held her by the shoulders, a little above him. Lori admired the way several kinds of tension transformed his arm muscles. Lovely.

'I took your proposition because I wanted you, not to discourage Justine. Although I have to admit it did cross my mind that that would be a side-benefit.'

'Two birds with one stone,' Lori said drily.

He grinned. 'And all your own idea. You weren't about to let yourself get involved with me, but you'd marry me. The logic escaped me, but I was damned if you were going to.' He gave a huff of laughter that bounced Lori off his rib-cage. 'It was all a face-saver for you and I called your bluff. No wonder you looked so stunned when I met you with the wedding plans all made.'

'You were very masterful,' she admitted with a glint in her eye. A masterful man who could bear watching. 'That wedding was my undoing.'

Fern shadows and bell-birds. Unqualified acceptance from his family and friends—affection. Lori remembered looking into his eyes as they'd stood here. At some deep level she'd known how it was even then. That was why she'd felt so emotional.

'You probably won't believe this, but I am quite—superstitious,' she said.

'Really?' said Haze gravely.

'Ever since I was small, I've felt that to make a promise and not keep it was to tempt the fates—bad luck. I imagined we'd have one of those quick ceremonies with the minimum of words, and instead I was making promises I'd never intended to make.'

Haze was silent for the count of six. 'We can have a proper ceremony, if you like, and you can choose the words you want to say—'

Lori looked shocked. 'Oh, no. It doesn't work like that. Once you've made promises you can't just rub them out like—like yesterday's trading figures at the Stock Exchange.' She smiled at the hint of trepidation in his eyes. 'We've had a proper wedding and I've made my promises.' She kissed him. 'And I intend to keep them.'

He manoeuvred on the narrow deck lounger until she was breathless beneath him. 'You know that soft spot I've got for you,' he murmured in her ear. 'A funny thing's happened...' He lowered himself squarely on her and Lori's eyes opened wide.

'Oh. I see,' she said.

There were the sounds of voices then, coming closer. Haze groaned. 'Oh, no. I forgot to phone them,' he said as a pram and three figures came into view on the path below the terrace. 'Robert's away. Jackie and the kids and my mother are coming to look after my place while I'm out with the students.'

Quickly they stood, just as three faces, framed in hats of varying shapes, looked up at them. 'Auntie Lori!' shrieked Amanda, and the ginger-freckled little girl came flying towards the house.

Home, Lori thought, standing with Haze's arm around her, wasn't a place. It was people. She waved to Meg and Jackie and looked into her husband's eyes. A special person. It was wherever love was.

It was Tate's traditional pre-Christmas cocktail party— an event that Lori used to dread. The Uncles were there, resplendent in dinner suits, and Mark, Carson and Fairlie.

'Hmm,' said Uncle Errol, inspecting Lori's short iridescent green dress with its several layers and quivering hems. 'Bit frivolous, isn't it, Lorelei? You are a director, after all. Look like a bimbo in that outfit, with your hair all...' He waggled his fingers to describe her crimped hair. 'What you need is something more dignified.'

Lori exchanged a glance with her husband.

'Lorelei,' said Uncle Clark, 'I hear you're meddling. Hoping to get a woman appointed to the board. Spare us the feminist stuff, please. You know we only want the best man for the job. What you need, young lady, is some sound guidance.' And he looked meaningfully at Haze, shot a glazed look of disapproval at the green dress and moved on.

Lori laughed, and in the press of people found herself solidly in her husband's arms. They looked into each other's eyes, relishing the thoughts secret between them. 'Our first Christmas alone together,' Lori said.

'And our last,' said Haze. 'Will we tell them now?'

'Let's not rush it. I want the photographer handy when we tell them that as from the next meeting they'll have a pregnant woman in the boardroom.'

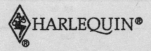

# Take 4 bestselling love stories FREE

## Plus get a FREE surprise gift!

## Special Limited-time Offer

**Mail to Harlequin Reader Service®**

3010 Walden Avenue
P.O. Box 1867
Buffalo, N.Y. 14240-1867

**YES!** Please send me 4 free Harlequin Presents® novels and my free surprise gift. Then send me 6 brand-new novels every month, which I will receive months before they appear in bookstores. Bill me at the low price of $2.90 each plus 25¢ delivery and applicable sales tax, if any*. That's the complete price and a savings of over 10% off the cover prices—quite a bargain! I understand that accepting the books and gift places me under no obligation ever to buy any books. I can always return a shipment and cancel at any time. Even if I never buy another book from Harlequin, the 4 free books and the surprise gift are mine to keep forever.

106 BPA A3UL

| Name | (PLEASE PRINT) | |
|------|----------------|---|
| Address | Apt. No. | |
| City | State | Zip |

This offer is limited to one order per household and not valid to present Harlequin Presents® subscribers. *Terms and prices are subject to change without notice. Sales tax applicable in N.Y.

UPRES-696

©1990 Harlequin Enterprises Limited

# *Harlequin Romance*

## celebrates forty fabulous years!

### Crack open the champagne and join us in celebrating Harlequin Romance's very special birthday.

**Forty years of bringing you the best in romance fiction—and the best just keeps getting better!**

Not only are we promising you three months of terrific books, authors and romance, but a chance to win a special hardbound 40th Anniversary collection featuring three of your favorite Harlequin Romance authors. And 150 lucky readers will receive an autographed collector's edition. Truly a one-of-a-kind keepsake.

Look in the back pages of any Harlequin Romance title, from April to June for more details.

### *Come join the party!*

# Free Gift Offer

With a Free Gift proof-of-purchase
from any Harlequin® book, you can receive
a beautiful cubic zirconia pendant.

This stunning marquise-shaped stone is a genuine cubic
zirconia—accented by an 18" gold tone necklace.
(Approximate retail value $19.95)

## Send for yours today...
## compliments of HARLEQUIN®

To receive your free gift, a cubic zirconia pendant, send us one original proof-of-purchase, photocopies not accepted, from the back of any Harlequin Romance®, Harlequin Presents®, Harlequin Temptation®, Harlequin Superromance®, Harlequin Intrigue®, Harlequin American Romance®, or Harlequin Historicals® title available at your favorite retail outlet, together with the Free Gift Certificate, plus a check or money order for $1.65 U.S./$2.15 CAN. (do not send cash) to cover postage and handling, payable to Harlequin Free Gift Offer. We will send you the specified gift. Allow 6 to 8 weeks for delivery. Offer good until December 31, 1997, or while quantities last. Offer valid in the U.S. and Canada only.

# Free Gift Certificate

Name: _____

Address: _____

City: _____ State/Province: _____ Zip/Postal Code: _____

Mail this certificate, one proof-of-purchase and a check or money order for postage and handling to: HARLEQUIN FREE GIFT OFFER 1997. In the U.S.: 3010 Walden Avenue, P.O. Box 9071, Buffalo NY 14269-9057. In Canada: P.O. Box 604, Fort Erie, Ontario L2Z 5X3.

---

## FREE GIFT OFFER                                        084-KEZ

ONE PROOF-OF-PURCHASE
To collect your fabulous FREE GIFT, a cubic zirconia pendant, you must include this original proof-of-purchase for each gift with the properly completed Free Gift Certificate.

---

084-KEZR